You're invited to a

CREEPOVER™

Read It and Weep!

by P. J. Night

SIMON SPOTLIGHT
New York London Toronto Sydney New Delhi

This book is a work of fiction. Any references to historical events, real people, or real locales are used fictitiously. Other names, characters, places, and incidents are the product of the author's imagination, and any resemblance to actual events or locales or persons, living or dead, is entirely coincidental.

SIMON SPOTLIGHT
An imprint of Simon & Schuster Children's Publishing Division
1230 Avenue of the Americas, New York, New York 10020
© 2013 by Simon & Schuster, Inc.
All rights reserved, including the right of reproduction in whole or in part in any form.
SIMON SPOTLIGHT and colophon are registered trademarks of Simon & Schuster, Inc.
YOU'RE INVITED TO A CREEPOVER is a trademark of Simon & Schuster, Inc.
Text by Sarah Albee
For information about special discounts for bulk purchases, please contact Simon & Schuster Special Sales at 1-866-506-1949 or business@simonandschuster.com.
Manufactured in the United States of America 0313 OFF
First Edition 10 9 8 7 6 5 4 3 2 1
ISBN 978-1-4424-5987-8
ISBN 978-1-4424-5988-5 (eBook)
Library of Congress Catalog Card Number 2013931742

CHAPTER 1

The babysitter checked the clock again. Past eleven. They'd promised they'd be home by ten thirty. She shifted sleepily in the deep leather chair and glanced back at the TV. She had it turned down low, to an old black-and-white movie, which was quaintly spooky. Practically every scene included ominous music, sinister characters wearing hats and trench coats, and lots of fog and shadows. But she wasn't the sort of girl that got scared easily.

Outside, the wind howled, rattling the old doors and window frames. The draft caused the heavy floor-to-ceiling drapes to billow, as though someone were hiding behind them. The rain streamed down the windows in rivulets.

Lightning flashed. For a brief instant, through the gap in the drapery, the girl could see the dark landscape illuminated outside—black trees bending, empty swings bobbing crazily in the wind. There was a loud crack of thunder.

And then the power went out.

With a blip the TV powered off. The reading lamp next to her went black. The girl was plunged into darkness, not complete blackness, but pretty close. With an exasperated sigh she stood up from the chair and groped her way toward the kitchen, shuffling with baby steps so as not to trip over any toys. Now she wished she'd done a better job of picking up after the twin girls, who'd been playing with their wooden food and plastic oven earlier that evening.

The kitchen was full of gray shadows and devoid of noise, except for the howling wind and pattering rain outside. There was no hum of the refrigerator. No whooshing of the dishwasher, which she'd actually remembered to turn on. Opening the drawer near the stove, she felt around for a flashlight. She came up with the next best thing—a candle, with a little holder attached. Luckily the gas stove worked, so she didn't have to search for matches and could light the candle. The weak flame flickered, shedding a wan light around her. And then she saw them:

A pair of green, glowing eyes, staring at her from the shadowy corner of the kitchen.

She gasped. Took a step backward, almost dropping the candle.

Then she exhaled.

"Nero! You dumb cat. You scared the life out of me."

She heard the orange-and-white tabby cat jump down from the counter and pad over to her, twining itself around her feet, purring.

Inside the pocket of her sweatshirt she felt her phone vibrate. She drew it out and checked the message. Another text.

I see you. You're in the kitchen. You're wearing a pink zip-up sweatshirt.

Her mouth went dry and her palms felt sweaty as she read the mysterious message. This was the third text she'd gotten tonight from that number. She scrolled back to reread the first two messages.

I'm back.

The second one was even creepier:

You thought you'd gotten rid of me. Well, you didn't. Your luck has changed.

This third one was deeply unsettling. She couldn't pass it off as a wrong number. She *was* wearing a pink sweatshirt. She *was* standing in the kitchen. How could someone possibly know that? She peered out of the window over the kitchen sink, straining her eyes to see past the streams of water running down. But all she could see was the blackness outside. All she could hear was the howling wind and the pattering rain. The kitchen faced the back of the house, where there was a small yard and then a grove of trees. No one in her right mind would be standing out there on a night like this. She set the candle down and texted back.

Whoever this is, cut it out. You're starting to freak me out.

Almost immediately, there was another text.

They're not coming home. Not anytime soon.

Fear eddied up and down her spine. Who was "they"? The twins' parents? She decided not to ask. This entire thing was as ridiculous as it was scary. She tried to convince herself that someone was just playing a practical joke on her. Her brothers or maybe her best friend.

A full two minutes passed without another text. The babysitter busied herself around the kitchen, trying to tidy it up as best she could in the darkness. Where were the twins' parents? Why hadn't they called her to say they'd be late?

And then she got another text.

I am in the basement.

Her breath caught in her throat. This really wasn't funny anymore. Suddenly she realized it wasn't someone playing a practical joke on her. No one she knew would do something like this. Play such a mean trick. She'd call her mom. And then maybe even 911. But when she looked at her phone again, she saw the worst possible message of all:

No service.

Wait. What was that sound?

Clomp. Clomp. Clomp.

At first she thought the sound was only in her imagination. But as it got louder, there was no mistaking the sound of footsteps. Then they stopped. She whirled around toward the basement door, which was shrouded in shadow. The door rattled. But that was the wind, wasn't it? Making it rattle?

She heard footsteps again, and a tiny, terrified whimper escaped from the back of her throat. Heavy footfalls continued making their way up the basement steps. And then slowly, ever so slowly, the knob on the basement door started to turn. When it opened, she saw what she'd been dreading—a figure covered in shadow. And then it started moving toward her.

CHAPTER 2

Charlotte Torres slammed the book closed, her heart pounding. What had possibly possessed her to check this book out of the library? She *hated* scary stories. Especially ones where people were trapped in the dark (and there was always someone trapped in the dark). She'd been afraid of the dark ever since she was a little kid, even though she would never, ever want to reveal such a baby-ish secret to anyone at her new middle school.

She'd gotten the book at the library earlier that afternoon. This red book. She had felt the strangest pull to it. Almost without knowing why she was doing it, she'd dragged a footstool over to a shelf in a shadowy back corner of the library, and then stepped onto the stool in order to reach this book on a shelf above her head. She'd had to stand on tippy-toe to pull it out and had almost lost her balance doing so.

And then once she had it, she hadn't even registered the section she was in or the title on the spine, which had almost completely worn away and was quite illegible. What had once most likely been a deep-red leather cover was now faded to almost pink, soft to the touch, like suede. She ran her hand over the book and then shivered. It was almost as though the book had chosen *her*. Like her feet had just carried her into the book stacks and her hand had dragged that step stool over and her whole unconscious self had made her climb up to get it.

A tiny voice inside Charlotte was issuing a warning. For such an old book, the story inside seemed so . . . now. Almost as though it could have been written about a girl like her. She ignored the voice and shoved the thought out of her mind.

She listened. The house had gone quiet. Her mom and the boys must be fast asleep in their rooms down the hall. She should be asleep too, but thanks to this stupid, scary book, she couldn't yet bring herself to turn out her light, even *with* the night-light blazing away in the corner.

She could remember exactly when she had become afraid of the dark. It was because of that incident at her cousins' house when she was only seven years old. Her mother was one of eight kids, so Charlotte had lots and lots of cousins, but this batch, the Kansas City batch, was her least favorite. They were her Uncle Ben's kids, three boys, all older, always playing some sport and arguing and tumbling over one another. They pulled her hair and teased her about her crooked teeth, and she absolutely hated being teased. It was so different in her own house, where Charlotte was the oldest. She helped her mom and dad look after her twin brothers, and she was practically never mean to them.

This set of cousins lived in a cul-de-sac in a big house. Even though she'd only been there twice in her life, Charlotte so vividly remembered their huge finished basement, where on cold or rainy days the three boys practically lived, playing pool, Ping-Pong, and video games. They even had a special room off the playroom, which was stocked with food, water, batteries, and a radio, just in case of tornadoes. That room had made an impression on her. At seven years old she'd already read

The Wizard of Oz and seen the movie, so she knew what a tornado was capable of doing. Uncle Ben referred to the room off the playroom as the "Twister Safe-Room."

The one major problem with the playroom—as all the kids knew—was that the light switch was located at the bottom of the basement steps. Which meant that if you were the last person to leave the basement, you had to turn the lights out at the bottom and then climb the stairs in the semidarkness. The basement was completely below ground, so there were no windows. The only light came from the open door at the top of the stairs. Charlotte always made sure she wasn't the last person in the basement. But on the third day of this particular visit her cousins Bobby and Ted had decided to play a trick on her. With a wink at one another they'd slammed their Ping-Pong paddles down on the table and then raced for the stairs. She'd been left alone, startled, as she was in the middle of working on a puzzle.

"Hey!" she yelled after them.

"Time for dinner. Last one up turns out the lights!" Bobby yelled over his shoulder, as he stampeded up the stairs behind Ted.

She jumped to her feet. She was not going to let them

call *her* a scaredy-cat. She marched over to the light switch and flicked it off. Then she turned to mount the stairs.

And that's when she realized the boys had closed the door at the top of the stairs, leaving her in complete blackness. She couldn't tell the difference with her eyes opened or closed.

Still, she would not let them upset her. She would be brave. Step by careful step, she felt her way up the stairs. She prayed they hadn't locked the door. The stairs seemed three times longer than she remembered them. What if she stepped on something in the dark? A snail? She shuddered to think of squishing one in her bare feet. Were there poisonous snakes in Kansas?

But finally she made it to the top. Put her hand on the knob.

And felt an icy hand clamp down on her shoulder from behind.

With a scream she jerked away and lost her footing, somehow turning around and falling feetfirst down the stairs, her bottom thud-thud-thudding until she came to rest halfway down, landing hard on her wrist. Pain and terror coiled inside her as she squeezed her eyes closed, waiting for whatever, whoever, was on the stairs with her.

But instead the grown-ups had thrown open the door. Light flooded the stairwell from above. There was no monster, or anything else, on the stairs when the grown-ups rescued her.

The boys had gotten into major trouble for what happened, of course. And she'd broken her wrist, which meant no swimming for the rest of that hot summer. She'd had nightmares for weeks afterward. But worst of all, she'd been afraid of the dark ever since. Even now, at age twelve and three quarters, she still slept with a night-light. She had never told anyone, not even her mom, about the icy hand on her shoulder that day. It was a terrible memory she kept deeply buried. One that she always reasoned away as a trick of her terrified imagination at that moment.

Charlotte shuddered and dropped the book on the floor next to her bed. Something bounced out. *Must be an old bookmark,* she thought. She'd return the book to the library tomorrow.

The best part about libraries, Charlotte had learned, was that she could practically always rely on them, like a beacon in a storm. Her dad was in the military, so her family moved constantly—five times since the twins were born. Before her mom had gone back to work, they'd spent many happy hours together at the library, wherever they happened to live. And now that she was old enough to walk places by herself, she knew she could find comfort, solace, and all the books she wanted at the library. Even before she made friends in a new town, books were always there to entertain her and fill up her days, and libraries were calm, comforting places. Librarians were practically always nice.

Charlotte and her family had only been living in this town outside Omaha, Nebraska, since July. The library had been the first place she'd explored. It was a beautiful, redbrick building from the nineteenth century, with huge windows that let in the sunlight, majestic shady trees on the front lawn, and plenty of big, comfy chairs for reading. It had that perfect library smell: a combination of old books, dusty pages, worn leather, and a pleasant mustiness. She'd fallen in love with it at once and found herself there several days a week. The librarian, Mrs. Lazer, learned her name after only her second visit.

But Mrs. Lazer had not been at the library this afternoon. A different librarian, an older man, someone she'd never seen before, had checked out her book, barely glancing at it. He muttered something about all the reshelving he had to do as he clapped the book closed and slid it across to Charlotte without even glancing at her.

She'd promised herself she wouldn't look at the book until she'd finished her homework. It would be her reward. All evening she had felt as though the book was calling to her. But because her mom had worked late tonight, she'd had to help the twins with their homework before she could even start her own, so she'd gotten to bed later than usual. She sighed in exasperation. After all that buildup, the book turned out to be scary. She *hated* scary stories.

She turned out the light and settled back into her pillow, trying to put the scary story out of her mind. Of all things, it had been a story about a girl her age who babysat. With the lights going out. It was almost as though it had been written especially to scare her. "Think happy thoughts," she told herself firmly. She opened one eye to be sure the night-light was working. It was.

Sleep did not come. Charlotte kept thinking back to what had happened at the library today. What was it about that book in particular that had been so compelling? She was again struck by the thought that the book had called to her, beckoning her to take it, to read it.

Suddenly Charlotte opened her eyes. She sat up in bed and flicked the light back on. She had that feeling again—an urgent, have-to-obey feeling that there was something she must do. But this time the feeling wasn't coming from the book. It was coming from the thing that had fallen *out* of it. She had to find it. Look at it. See what it was. She swung her legs around and got out of bed. Where was it? She was sure she'd seen it on the floor next to her bed.

She got down on hands and knees and looked under the bed. There were still a couple of garbage bags full of winter clothes that she hadn't yet unpacked, even after months in her new room. The thing that had fallen out of the book wasn't there. She sat back. Had she only thought she'd seen something? Maybe she'd imagined it.

Her eyes came to rest on a rectangular-shaped thing resting on her bedside table. She leaned toward it and reached for it. It was a card.

How odd, she thought. She'd seen it fall onto the floor. Maybe she'd fallen asleep briefly, and her mother had come in, picked it up, and placed it on the table next to her bed. But the nagging little voice told her that wasn't possible.

She peered closely at it. It felt stiff and heavy in her hand, much stiffer than a playing card or an index card. Almost as inflexible as if it were made of thin wood or something. It was bigger than an ordinary playing card too.

She studied the picture on it. In the center of the card was a round orange shape, crisscrossed with measurement lines of some sort. It looked sort of like a compass, except that instead of north-south-east-west indications there were odd symbols. It was set against a blue background with floating gray clouds, and in each corner of the card was a winged horselike creature, each one a little different from the next. At the bottom of the card, in old-fashioned type, Charlotte read the words WHEEL OF FORTUNE. She turned the card over. On the back was a twirly, intricate design, almost like the pattern on an Oriental carpet. And something was written—handwritten—in old-fashioned, spidery script, diagonally across the back. She brought the card closer to the light, and squinted at it.

Pass this along or you'll be sorry.

Pass *what* along, she wondered, turning the card over and then back again. The card? Was this some person's idea of a dumb chain message? She despised those, the ones that urged her to forward the e-mail to ten people or she'd have bad luck, or whatever. Her cousin Sheila was always sending them to her, apologizing but saying she didn't dare break them because she was superstitious. Well, Charlotte wasn't. She usually deleted them promptly. If it was a chain message, it was a strange way to receive it. After all, putting a message in an old library book wasn't the fastest way to communicate. She put the card inside the book again and placed them both carefully on her bedside table. Then she turned out the light and went back to sleep.

And plunged right into a nightmare.

CHAPTER 3

Running, running, but her legs felt so heavy. It was dark. Nighttime, with a wan gray light where the moon shone feebly behind rushing clouds. The gloom hung heavy. Fog swirled around her. What was chasing her? Something terrible. Something just out of sight, in the swirling darkness, something that was intent on harming her. Not knowing what her pursuer looked like seemed almost scarier. She knew only that she must get away.

Now she was running barefoot through cold, muddy, slimy stuff. Her pajamas were soaked from the mist. She sloshed through the swampy marsh. Who knew what lurked in that sucking mud? Her legs could hardly move. Every leaden step was a huge effort. Her bare feet squelched unpleasantly.

The thing—her pursuer—was gaining on her. She could hear it just behind her, running through the mud in big, sucking gulps. Now she could feel its hot, stifling breath on the back of her neck. She smelled something foul: putrid and rotten and sickly sweet all at the same time. And then it grabbed her, an icy hand on her shoulder, just like what had happened so many years ago on her cousins' basement steps.

She fell down, face-first, into the stinking, slimy mud. She couldn't breathe. Something was holding her face down in the muck. She was going to drown, to suffocate. She tried to scream.

And woke up with her head buried in the pillow.

It was morning.

She could smell coffee brewing. Her mother was up, of course. Charlotte glanced at the clock. Six forty-five. The alarm wasn't due to go off for fifteen more minutes. She groaned and swung her feet out of bed. That was the last time she was going to read a scary story before bed. In fact it was the last time she would read a scary story, period.

She dressed quickly, pausing to frown at herself in the mirror. Her brown hair spiraled down past her shoulders in a wildly unkempt way. She gathered it up and tied it back with a hair elastic. Her braces glinted at her in the mirror. Why had she inherited each of her parents' flaws and none of their good traits? She'd gotten her father's unruly hair, but not his startling blue eyes or his ramrod-straight military posture. She'd inherited her mom's crooked teeth, but not her glossy hair or her graceful, willowy figure. It wasn't fair. Her twin brothers had gotten good teeth and perfect, shiny hair. She sighed as she adjusted her father's framed photo on her dresser. He looked so handsome in his air force uniform. It had been a month since he'd been deployed to the Middle East. She felt the usual pang of worry in the pit of her stomach that she always did when she thought about her dad, which was often.

At least she'd inherited her parents' intelligence, she had to admit. It was nice not to have to struggle to understand everything, the way her friend Alicia, at her last school, had. She wondered how Alicia was doing. She hadn't heard from her in a while. Well. That was normal. It wasn't easy to maintain long-term friendships when you moved eight times in twelve years. She felt lucky to have met Lauren at her new school. And to have access to such an awesome public library.

Her eyes fell on the red book next to her bed. Not that she was superstitious, but the last thing she needed was to worry about bad luck. She picked the book up and slipped the card from its pages. She'd return the book to the library after school today. Then she tucked the card into a pocket of her backpack.

In the hallway outside her room she could hear her eight-year-old brothers running full speed toward the stairs. *A herd of elephants would sound quieter,* she thought, rolling her eyes. Where did they get all this energy so early in the morning? They were always having contests, racing each other to be the first one to get to the breakfast table, or arguing about who got the last cookie or whose turn it was to sit next to the window on the bus. *It must be exhausting to be a twin,* Charlotte thought, not for the first time. After all, it was exhausting to live with them.

She was halfway down the stairs when she heard her mother call to her from her bedroom.

"Charlotte, did you put the boys' soccer uniforms in the wash last night like I asked you?"

"Yep!" she called back.

"Thanks, honey! Can you run them in the dryer so they'll be ready for the twins' game tonight?"

"Yep!" Charlotte called back, and ran downstairs to the laundry room. She liked being a help to her mom, who'd gone back to work for the first time since the twins were born. With her dad gone, Charlotte knew her mom was counting on her for a lot of help. Especially with the twins' math homework. Her mom was really smart, just not at math—even third-grade math.

When she opened the washer to transfer the load to the dryer, she froze, staring into the washing machine.

The mostly white load she'd put in the night before had turned pink.

Then she remembered throwing her new red sweatshirt in with the rest of the load. She began pulling out the damp, wrinkled clothes. She tugged a soccer jersey from the clump and held it up.

It was decidedly pink.

Maybe the pink will drain out somehow in the drying process, she thought, although deep down she knew that wasn't really possible. This day had not started out well.

Her mom was in her nurse's scrubs when Charlotte

dragged her feet into the kitchen a few minutes later. Her brothers were noisily arguing about which of two European soccer teams was better. Charlotte was pretty sure neither boy had ever even watched these teams play. But while they were busy arguing, she took the opportunity to speak quietly to her mother over near the stove.

"Mom, I kind of turned the twins' uniforms a little bit pink. With my new sweatshirt," she murmured into her mother's ear, casting her eyes downward.

Her mother let out an exasperated sigh. "Oh, Char. I thought we went over all that when I showed you how to do laundry. How to separate the whites."

Charlotte mumbled "sorry" under her breath.

"I'll try to bleach them later. But I'm working a double shift. I'm only home for an hour or so this afternoon, and then I have to go back to the hospital. Your brothers are not going to be happy about this," said her mother wearily.

"Not going to be happy about what?" asked Jon. He and Thomas had suddenly gone quiet.

"Nothing," said Charlotte quickly.

"What did she do, Mom?" demanded Thomas suspiciously.

"Nothing!" said Charlotte again. "I just messed up on the laundry a little, but Mom can fix it. Right, Mom?"

Her mother glared at her. "Help them make sure they're all packed up for the bus," she said. "I'll make sure the dryer's off before I leave for the hospital."

"What happened to the laundry?" asked Thomas suspiciously. "Did something shrink or something?"

"No. Everything's fine. Now go get packed up," said Charlotte, hustling them toward the front hallway.

Later that morning, in homeroom, Charlotte slid into her desk next to her new friend, Lauren Kowalski. Lauren had been new the year before, in sixth grade. She wasn't a military kid, though. Her dad was a science professor at the university. Lauren's mom had died a long time ago. Charlotte had met Lauren on the first day of school, in math class.

"Everyone sit tight," called Mrs. Benedict. "I have to run to the copier for a few minutes. Work on your homework. You must have *something* you didn't finish."

"Actually, I finished mine," Charlotte said to Lauren in a low voice.

"Yeah, I finished all mine, too," said Lauren.

"So," Charlotte began, thinking of something to talk about to pass the time, "I had the weirdest dream last night." She told Lauren about her nightmare.

"Sounds freaky. All those shadows and fog and stuff. Are you scared of the dark?" asked Lauren, perceptive as usual.

Charlotte was caught off guard. "Me? No! I—well, yeah I guess a little. How did you know?"

"Dreams are your hopes and fears, or that's what my aunt Marina tells me," said Lauren. "If it was that scary, it sounds like your subconscious mind went straight to the place it prefers to avoid."

Charlotte shifted uncomfortably in her seat. She'd never told anyone about her fear of the dark. And she didn't really know Lauren all that well. School had only started a few weeks ago. But she really liked her so far. Lauren seemed so confident. And smart. No-nonsense. Lauren was tall and angular. She dressed in offbeat, retro attire that wasn't especially trendy but always looked cool. Charlotte had noticed that Lauren did well in school, hung out with the smart kids, and wasn't afraid to say what was on her mind. She also didn't seem to care about where she stood on the popularity scale.

It was kind of refreshing. "So, um, are *you* afraid of anything?" Charlotte asked her.

"Spiders," said Lauren immediately. "Hate 'em. I know it's irrational. My dad's an arachnologist, and—"

"What's that?"

"A scientist who studies spiders and stuff," she said. "And he's always telling me how great spiders are, and how they're really beneficial in the food web and all that, but I just can't stand all those legs and the creepy-crawly way they walk, and the way they survive, sucking the guts out of living insects." She shuddered, and her short, shiny hair bounced around her shoulders. "When I was little, I was at this camp called Playland Camp, and we were hanging around in this meadow on a field trip to a farm. I climbed a tree and collided with a huge web of newly hatched baby spiders. They crawled all over me. I was so freaked out I actually fell out of the tree. I didn't hurt myself, but I still haven't recovered from the trauma."

Charlotte laughed sympathetically, relieved that Lauren hadn't made fun of her for her phobia, and wishing she could be as frank and unembarrassed as her new friend. Then she remembered the card. She pulled it out of the pocket of her backpack.

"Can I show you something weird? I found it yesterday. In a book. Do you have any idea what this is?" she asked Lauren.

Lauren took the card and peered at it, frowning. Her wide-set eyes and pouty lips didn't quite fit her face, but Charlotte suspected her features would all come together by the time she was a teenager. Braces and a gawky frame and unevenly proportioned features on a twelve-year-old looked like they might easily translate to supermodel good looks on a teenager. Now, though, she was a misfit like Charlotte. Smart, nerdy, awkwardly angular.

"Where'd you get this?" asked Lauren, turning it over and reading the message scrawled across the back.

"Inside a library book," said Charlotte. "Weird, isn't it?"

"Well, yes and no," said Lauren matter-of-factly. "It's weird because it looks really old, like, from the middle ages or something. But I think it's just a tarot card, actually."

"What's a tarot card?"

"People use them to tell fortunes," she said with a shrug. "I don't know much about them, but I have seen them before. At my aunt's house. And I don't know what this particular card means. Of course I don't believe in any of that mumbo jumbo stuff, but I can show it to my aunt Marina if you want. She lives right near here."

"You mean you are actually related to someone who can tell fortunes? I thought everyone in your family was into science like you," said Charlotte.

Lauren grinned. "They are, but it's not like I'm from a huge family. My dad's a scientist, and his brother Jack, the one who died in a car accident a few years ago, was a scientist too. Marina is my aunt by marriage. She was married to Uncle Jack. She still lives in the house the two of them used to live in when they were married."

"Does she have any kids?"

"Never wanted any. But I think she feels like she needs to mother me because she knows it's just my dad and me, and I guess my dad is a lot like Jack. Sort of an absentminded professor type, and she knows that. And also because I have an artsy side."

Charlotte nodded, and Lauren went back to studying the card and shrugged. "I'll ask Aunt Marina," she said.

Suddenly someone behind Lauren snatched the card from her hand.

"Hey!" said Lauren.

Charlotte wheeled around.

"What's this? You two geeks into fortune telling now?"

It was Stacy Matthews, the most popular and stuck-up girl in seventh grade. Behind her stood Ava and Maddy, giggling as usual.

"It's nothing," said Charlotte and Lauren simultaneously.

Stacy raised her eyebrow. Then she looked down at the card. "Looks like some weird Goth thing," she said. She tossed the card back down on the desk, having evidently lost interest.

Charlotte picked it up and shoved it into her bag.

"So did you guys finish the math homework for today or what?"

Lauren and Charlotte darted a look at each other.

"Yeah," said Charlotte warily.

Stacy waited, hands on hips. "So can I borrow yours to check my answers?"

"I don't have mine on me right now," said Lauren.

"Me neither," said Charlotte, giving Stacy a little smile. Which was only a partial untruth. It wasn't on her exactly. It was inside her backpack, under the desk.

Stacy's eyes narrowed. "Well thanks anyway," she

said in a voice that meant she felt the exact opposite. "Hey, have you ever thought about closing your mouth when you smile, Charlotte?"

Charlotte could feel her cheeks turn red. She shook her head.

"Whatever. Listen. We need to help each other," Stacy continued. "This accelerated math class we're in together is super ridiculous. I'm going to be a singer, so what do I need math for, right? So why don't we make a deal? You can help me with the math homework, and I'll give you some fashion advice, which you are badly in need of—no offense."

Before Charlotte had time to respond, Mrs. Benedict returned to class and flicked the lights on and off, which the kids knew meant it was time to get back to their seats for announcements. Stacy flounced back to her chair.

"Why is she like that?" whispered Charlotte, staring at Stacy in disbelief.

"I guess she really thinks she's above everyone," whispered Lauren. "And why wouldn't she? She is star of the girls' basketball team. Actress. Singer. And she's going out with Julian Wilson. But whatever. She despises me now because I got the role of Adelaide in *Guys and Dolls*, which she really wanted. She's got a great role in the school musical too, but she really wanted to be Adelaide."

Charlotte frowned. "I don't like the idea of her copying off me," she said. "But she looks like somebody to watch out for." Charlotte had been at enough schools to learn to recognize these people.

Announcements droned on, but finally the bell rang, and everyone filed out and headed for their next class.

It wasn't until after they'd parted that Charlotte realized she'd forgotten to pass the card to Lauren.

CHAPTER 4

Charlotte didn't take the bus home after school. She decided to walk so she could stop by the library to return that awful book.

She peered in through the window as she approached the library.

Nice Mrs. Lazer was still not at her desk in the reference room. The same grumpy librarian from yesterday was there.

The book return bin was located just outside the front door. Just as Charlotte had clanged the bin closed, the library door opened, and Mrs. Drayton came out. She was the mother of one of Charlotte's new acquaintances at school.

"Oh, hello, Charlotte," she said. "Awful thing about Mrs. Lazer, isn't it?"

"Mrs. Lazer? The librarian? I didn't hear. What happened?" asked Charlotte.

"She slipped off a stool two days ago when she was reshelving a book on one of the high shelves," said Mrs. Drayton. "I think she'll be all right, but they want her off her feet for a while. See you soon, I hope!"

No wonder she hadn't seen Mrs. Lazer lately. Charlotte considered going inside to look for a new book, but then decided she didn't feel like it. Not today. Not with the grumpy substitute librarian in there. Maybe she'd get ahead on her English homework tonight instead. They were reading *A Midsummer Night's Dream*, the play by Shakespeare.

As she stood there, ready to head home, she realized she didn't have her copy of the play. She'd left it in her locker in her haste to get going.

"Aw, man," she said out loud. She knew her mom wanted her home soon, because she was working at the hospital tonight, and she wanted Charlotte to help the twins with their homework. Charlotte decided to take the shortcut back to school to get her book, which meant going back through the patch of woods behind the library. On the other side of the woods were the baseball field and the back of the middle school.

Charlotte trotted down the front steps and then headed around to the back, behind the library, toward the woods. She found the narrow path, but the footing was uneven and not very well maintained. It was only a short distance—about half the size of the school's football field—through the little patch of trees, but Charlotte was surprised at how quickly the woods closed around her, as though she were in the middle of the wilderness. She picked up the pace.

The wan, late-afternoon sun glinted through the branches overhead, but rather suddenly the sun seemed to go behind a cloud, and a chilly gloom slipped in. The woods grew dark and shadowy. A wind sprang up, whipping her hair around her face, across her eyes, into her mouth.

Suddenly she heard her name.

Charlotte.

It was whispered and seemed to be coming from all around her. Maybe it was only the wind. Her mind was playing tricks on her. Yes. Definitely the wind.

Charlotte!

"Who's there?" she called, slowing to a stop.

There was no answer.

A cold stab of fear struck her. She knew she was closer to the other side of the wooded area than where she'd entered, so she proceeded straight, beginning to run, her backpack bouncing on her back.

I'm coming for youuuuu!

Now she was sprinting full speed and praying she wouldn't trip over the uneven terrain and the many roots and brambles in her path. It was so dark in this wood. At any minute she expected the same cold hand to land on her shoulder, just like in her cousins' basement.

The path curved slightly to the left, and she saw a dimly-lit patch of grass ahead. The baseball field. Don't trip. Don't trip. Don't trip.

Charrrrrrrrlooooooooote!

She burst out of the woods and onto the baseball field, panting and whimpering.

And almost ran smack into Lauren.

"Charlotte? What's up? What's the matter? You look awful!"

"Lauren!" said Charlotte, relief flooding through her.

"I just—I thought—" She stopped herself. She couldn't tell Lauren what had just happened. The last thing she needed was for her new friend to think she was hearing voices. "Nothing," she said. "I just forgot—"

"*A Midsummer Night's Dream?*" Lauren interrupted, holding the book up. "I know. You left it on your desk in social studies. I just finished play rehearsal and was on my way to bring it to you. And to pick up that card you wanted me to show to my aunt."

Charlotte smiled. Her heartbeat was slowing to a normal pace now. She must have imagined the voice in the woods. "Thank you so much. That's awesome." She took the book, dug the card out of her bag, and handed it to Lauren.

Lauren shoved the card into her bag and tilted her head to the side, scrutinizing Charlotte closely. "You sure you're okay? You look really pale and freaked out."

"I'm fine," said Charlotte. "Thanks again for the book."

The twins were sitting at the kitchen table, doing homework, when Charlotte walked in.

"Charlotte! Can you help us with integers?" asked

Thomas, before Charlotte had even closed the door.

"Hello, yourself," said Charlotte, swinging her heavy backpack off her shoulders and plunking it into an empty chair.

Their mom came bustling into the kitchen, her head down as she finished tying the waistband of her nursing scrubs. She looked up and almost collided with Charlotte.

"Oh! Hi, honey!" She turned toward the twins. "Jonathan, Thomas, run up and get changed. The Kenersons will be here in a half hour to bring you to the game. I've got sandwiches and waters on the counter."

"Mom, can I have a smartphone?" asked John, sliding back from the table and heading for the door.

Their mother let out a guffaw. "Yeah, sure. As *if*."

Thomas rolled his eyes at his brother. "Dude, nice try!"

Their mom picked up her pocketbook. "I have to get back to the hospital. Good luck in your game, you two. I'll be home late, so Char's in charge."

She gave Charlotte a quick kiss on the cheek and grabbed her keys.

"Hey," said Charlotte. "Any word from Daddy?"

Her mother paused with her hand on the knob.

She turned to Charlotte and shook her head quickly.

"It's been three days," said Charlotte, as though her mother didn't know that. She could tell the boys were listening too, by the way they'd stopped at the door.

"I know. But he did tell us it might be hard to communicate for a few days, remember?"

Charlotte nodded, regarding her mother carefully. She was getting good at assessing her mother's face to see just how worried, or not worried, she was. She didn't seem unusually worried, Charlotte noted with relief. And it wasn't like her dad was in combat. He just fixed stuff, like things inside of airplanes. Of course he was fine.

"He'll be home soon," said her mother with a determinedly cheerful smile. "Bye, guys."

Three minutes later, Charlotte heard a howl from upstairs, followed by a second howl.

"They're *pink*!" yelled Jon.

"*Bright* pink!" added Thomas.

Charlotte groaned. The soccer uniforms. She'd forgotten about turning them pink. Her mom must have forgotten too.

The twins came stomping into the kitchen. Charlotte had to acknowledge that there was a definite pink tint to their white uniforms, and their socks were even pinker.

"You guys look fine," said Charlotte brightly. "No one will notice. Mom can bleach them this weekend. It's only one game."

Charlotte and the boys worked on their homework for a few minutes before Charlotte heard a toot from a car horn in the driveway.

"They're here," she said, and, shoving the twins' bags into their hands, she propelled them out the door.

As soon as her brothers had left, Charlotte called Lauren. "Hey," Charlotte said. "Thanks again for bringing me the book."

"You're welcome," said Lauren, not sounding like her usual enthusiastic self. "Now you can return the favor. What are the pages of social studies that we're supposed to read tonight?"

"I can check," said Charlotte. Cradling the phone under her chin, she pulled out her planner. "Pages 167 to 172," she said. "How come you don't have your planner?"

"Forgot it," said Lauren. "Must have left it in my locker. I *never* leave stuff in my locker."

"Yeah. You *never* leave stuff in your locker. I'm the

one who usually leaves stuff lying around and calls *you*," agreed Charlotte.

"Yes, it's been quite the exciting afternoon since I last saw you," said Lauren. "My dad got a speeding ticket. And the whole reason he was speeding, even though he was barely speeding, was that he was late for a meeting for some grant thing he applied for. So he missed the meeting. And now he's worried he's not going to get the grant. *And* as I was walking home from school today, a guy walking his dog suddenly decided to stop dead in the middle of the sidewalk to send a text, and I smacked right into him and we both went flying."

"Oh no!" said Charlotte. "Are you okay?"

"Fine," said Lauren shortly. "Just feel stupid is all. And while I was lying on the ground, the stupid dog slobbered all over me. I've washed my face three times. Honestly, there should be a law against texting on the sidewalk."

Charlotte told Lauren about her brothers' pink uniforms.

"That's bad," agreed Lauren. "They're pretty much never going to live that one down. Which means they'll probably never forgive you."

"Thanks for being so uplifting," said Charlotte drily.

"So did you have a chance to ask your aunt about that card?"

"No, I couldn't today. I called her just as she was going off somewhere for the evening. She said she won't be back until late. I'll head over there tomorrow after rehearsal."

"Okay—watch out for texting dog walkers!" joked Charlotte. She clicked off her phone.

CHAPTER 5

The next morning Lauren woke up having trouble breathing. She felt intense pressure on her chest. What was happening? Her mind was still groggy with sleep. Her eyes opened.

Teddy, her dog, was sitting on her stomach, panting cheerfully.

She groaned and rolled over, causing him to scrabble to regain his footing on top of her hip. She peered at the clock. It was only five fifteen!

"Teddy! It's too early!" She tried to shove him off the bed, but he jumped right back up again. This was his way of saying he needed to go outside.

Why hadn't he bothered her dad? He usually walked

Teddy in the morning. That was the arrangement they had. Her dad kept odd hours, but he almost always woke up early. Lauren walked Teddy in the late afternoon, when she got home from play rehearsal. Lauren also made dinner most nights. She was probably the only middle schooler on the planet who'd actually gotten sick of pizza. Because her dad couldn't cook anything except scrambled eggs, she'd learned to make quite a few things. She was getting pretty good. She wasn't ready to be a TV chef yet, but she wasn't bad.

She rolled out of bed, scooped Teddy up in her arms, and padded toward her dad's room. His bed was empty and looked like he hadn't slept in it at all.

She found him downstairs at his desk. The desk lamp was still on, and he was asleep, his unshaven cheek resting on his arm, which was draped across his notebook.

"Dad?" she said, shaking him gently by the arm.

He woke up almost at once, massaging his face with his open palms as though trying to get the circulation going again.

"Lauren! What time is it?" he asked.

"Too early for me to get up," she said, dumping Teddy on the desk in front of him. "He wants to go outside."

Her dad stood up. He was still fully dressed from the night before. "Okay, honey, I'll take him," he mumbled. He pulled his sport coat off the back of his chair, shrugged his arms into it, and headed out with Teddy.

As Lauren trudged back upstairs for a couple more hours of sleep, she wished, for perhaps the thousandth time, that her father didn't work so much. Maybe then he'd have time to meet someone who would make sure he didn't sleep in his clothes at his desk all night. It was just a little too much responsibility for her.

Lauren ended up oversleeping. She woke up to the sound of her iPod playing and wondered how long she'd been listening to it in her dreams. With one eye she saw that it was nearly seven thirty. Ten minutes to get to the bus.

She leaped out of bed, threw on some clothes, and hastily packed up her stuff. As she passed into the kitchen to grab a bagel, she saw that her father had fallen back asleep, this time on the living room couch. Teddy was curled up next to him. He stirred, just as she had her hand on the front door.

"Have a good day, honey," he said, his words still slurred with sleepiness.

"Thanks," she said. "How come you fell asleep at your desk?"

He sat up, dumping Teddy to the floor. "I got turned down for my grant proposal, so I'm working on revising it and trying for another one," he admitted. "The deadline's looming, and I haven't been able to replicate my results. I still have a lot of data to analyze."

Lauren nodded. "Sorry about that, Daddy," she said. "I'll be home tonight to take Teddy out and make supper."

As she trudged to the bus stop, she pondered her father's situation. The week before, he'd been so excited, telling her he was on the verge of a breakthrough. And now he looked so disappointed. What bad luck.

She looked both ways before turning onto the sidewalk from her front walkway. She never knew if some skateboarder would be bearing down on her from any direction in this neighborhood. Or if a dog walker might happen along who was texting and not looking where he was going.

It started raining when she was halfway to the bus stop. Too late to turn around and go home for an umbrella. Great.

This was not just a drizzle. Fat, heavy drops

immediately darkened the pavement. It was promising to be a downpour. She swiveled her backpack around to the front and put her arms through the straps backward, trying to keep it more or less dry under her cardigan sweater. She wondered if it would occur to her dad to notice that it was raining and give her a ride to school so she wouldn't have to wait for the bus. Doubtful. He tended not to notice stuff like rain when he was in the middle of a big project.

Luckily the bus arrived pretty quickly, and she sank gratefully into a seat in the middle. She usually sat by herself for two stops before Gwen got on and joined her. Gwen Drayton was in her English and Spanish classes. Last year when Lauren had been the new kid, Gwen had gone out of her way to be friendly, even inviting Lauren to join her at the smart kids' table in the cafeteria. And even though Gwen was the kind of annoying smart kid who always moaned about how she was sure she'd failed every test they took and then later sheepishly admitted to acing it, Lauren had to admit that Gwen was pretty great. She had also been super-welcoming to Charlotte when Lauren had introduced her to the smart-kid group this year.

Still, for two stops before Gwen got on, Lauren

had to endure the nonstop chatter behind her, coming from stuck-up Stacy and her stuck-up friends, Ava and Maddy, and their incessant giggling and gossiping and squealing.

Lauren remembered, happily, that she'd packed her iPod. That was just the thing to drown out the girls behind her. She was rummaging through her backpack looking for it, when she felt something light, but disconcertingly ticklish, drop from above onto her neck and then skitter down the inside of her shirt.

She shot up from her seat, plucking her shirt out and away from her body with two fingers and shaking it frantically in order to dislodge what had fallen inside it. This was one of those rare times when she was glad she didn't yet need to wear a bra, because the insect, or whatever it was, came right out of the bottom of her shirt and plopped onto the seat next to her.

It turned out to be a large, hairy, disgusting spider. She shrieked twice—two terrified, high-pitched squeaks.

And then realized the thing was made of rubber.

The bus driver remained oblivious to what was going on, because Lauren's squeaks had coincided almost perfectly with the screech of the bus's brakes as it slowed down for the next stop. Lauren sat back down quickly.

Peals of giggles erupted behind her. Lauren felt rage boil up inside, but she managed to contain it, barely. She picked up the spider between two fingers. Even though she knew it was made of rubber, the thing was pretty realistic and still loathsome to the touch.

"Really funny," she said to the three girls, who were all holding their stomachs and pointing and laughing.

"Got ya!" taunted Stacy.

"Did you see her jump?" Maddy asked Ava.

"I totally saw her jump," answered Ava.

"I wasn't scared," said Lauren stiffly. "Just startled."

"As if," scoffed Stacy, tossing her hair. "You've been scared of spiders ever since Playland Camp days."

"Why? What happened at Playland Camp?" asked Ava eagerly.

"Remember, Laur-Laur?" coaxed Stacy.

Lauren gave her a huge fake smile, then she swiveled back around in her seat. She could hear the three girls whispering to one another, no doubt having a big guffaw over what had happened so many years ago. What were the chances that she and Stacy would have known each other for one brief summer, so many years ago? Lauren and her dad had been living in California at the time, but that one summer Lauren had come to Nebraska to stay with her aunt Marina and uncle Jack while her father was off on a research trip to Costa Rica. That was the summer she had her brush with the spider's nest, and Stacy had been there to witness the whole thing. Aunt Marina had been really sweet about it. She'd held her and soothed her just like her mother might have, and that had been the beginning of the special bond between the two of them, which they'd had ever since. But still. The experience had traumatized her. That was six years ago. Why did Stacy have to be a part of that awful incident? Of all people.

Suddenly someone slid into the seat next to her. It was Stacy.

"Guess what, Laur-Laur?" said Stacy in that same fake-sweet, mocking voice. She dropped her voice to a whisper. "I got the whole thing on my phone." She held up her phone, which displayed a paused video. The still shot showed Lauren bending over her backpack. Stacy must have slid into the empty seat across from Lauren without Lauren's being aware of it and filmed the whole spider thing.

"So what?" said Lauren with a shrug, acting as hard as she possibly could to pretend she didn't care when, in fact, she really cared a lot. What would Stacy do with such a video? The possibilities for evil were vast.

"Yeah, there is no need to worry about this video. I promise, pinky-swear, not to send it to everyone in the middle school."

"Good," said Lauren, and she meant it.

"Although it is tempting, considering the pink undies with the blue butterflies you have on today."

Lauren's blood ran cold. How did Stacy know?

"You could totally see the tops of them when you were hollering and tugging at your shirt just a minute ago," said Stacy, still in that sweet tone.

Of course today had to be the day she'd worn her oldest and ugliest pair of underwear. She hadn't done laundry in forever because of how busy she'd been with play rehearsals. These had been the last pair in her drawer.

She knew as well as anyone in middle school that if her classmates saw this video she would never, ever hear the end of it.

"Yep, I won't show the video around at all," Stacy

continued. "Provided of course that you help me with this week's lab report."

Lauren blinked at her. "The lab report," she echoed.

"Mmm-hmm. Actually, you can help me with *all* the science labs from now on," said Stacy.

So it was blackmail.

The bus hissed to a stop and Gwen clomped up the steps, decked out head to toe in matching raincoat, rain hat, rain boots, and umbrella.

"Here comes your friend, Paddington Bear," said Stacy. "I'll leave you two alone. Think about what I said, Laur-Laur." She slid out of the seat and resumed her place at the back of the bus, where Lauren heard a round of fresh giggling. With one eyebrow raised in curiosity, Gwen slid into the seat next to Lauren.

"What was that about?" she asked Lauren curiously.

Lauren shrugged. "Nothing. Just Stacy being her usual charming self."

CHAPTER 6

The rest of school that day was pretty uneventful. Lauren had several periods with Charlotte—homeroom, math, and social studies—but Charlotte had to work the student council bake sale during lunch, so they didn't have a chance to talk much until social studies, just before the second bell rang.

"I'm going to Aunt Marina's after rehearsal today," Lauren said to Charlotte. "I told her I have something 'weird and mystical' to show her." She made air quotes with her fingers to show she didn't really buy into all that stuff surrounding the card.

Charlotte had a weird look on her face. Kind of uneasy. She gave a forced laugh. "I don't believe the card is anything special," she said. "But it might just be cool to find out more about it."

By the time rehearsal was over, the rain had mostly stopped. Aunt Marina texted Lauren to see whether she wanted a ride, but as she lived close to school, Lauren told her she would walk.

From the outside, Aunt Marina's house looked pretty ordinary, much like the other houses on the block. Small but comfortable, with a modest front lawn and a center walkway leading to the front steps. The one feature that made Aunt Marina's house stand out was her flower garden, which was always a riot of color.

Aunt Marina had left the door unlocked, and Lauren knew it was fine to walk in. It smelled spicy inside—a combination of cinnamon, sandalwood, and patchouli. The interior of the house was a jumble of colors: oranges, pinks, and aquas. Lots of beaded curtains, colorful floor cushions, and funky knickknacks that Aunt Marina had collected during her world travels.

"In here!" She heard her aunt call from the living room.

Aunt Marina was standing on her head, her bare feet pointed up toward the ceiling, in a complicated-looking yoga pose, her face pink, her long blond hair tumbled around her arms.

"Hi, Aunt Marina," Lauren greeted her. She was just heading toward the couch when a black streak stopped her in her tracks. "Hey, Cinder," she said to Aunt Marina's cat. "You almost tripped me, as usual."

Cinder sat with his tail curled around his feet, staring without blinking at Lauren. Then he thrust out his paw and began grooming it.

"Hey, isn't it bad luck to have a black cat cross your path?" asked Lauren with a wink, and then plopped down on the couch and helped herself to a spiced wasabi pea from the dish on the coffee table.

"If it is, then I'm in big trouble," said Aunt Marina, her voice curiously muffled by being upside down, "because he walks in front of me about five times a day."

"Lucky for us we don't believe in that silly superstition," Lauren added.

Aunt Marina's feet flipped forward and she rolled gracefully up to a standing position. She was a petite person, an inch or so shorter than Lauren, and very young-looking for her age. Lauren supposed it was because she didn't have any kids. All that worrying seemed to make parents go gray early.

"Hello, darlin'," said Aunt Marina, bending over to hug Lauren and then flopping onto the couch next to her. "Everyone should get upside down for a little piece of every day. It's so good for the circulation and the joints. So what's this thing you said you wanted to show me?"

Lauren pulled the card out of her bag and handed it to Aunt Marina.

Aunt Marina scrutinized the card. "Wow, this is pretty cool. It's a very old tarot card. You don't see many like this anymore." She chuckled when she saw the message written on the back of the card. "Someone has an odd sense of humor," she remarked.

"Do you know what the card means?" asked Lauren.

"It's the Wheel of Fortune card," she said. "From the cracks and bends in the paper, it looks like this card is pretty old. As for the message on the back, I wouldn't worry about it. Chain messages are just a bunch of mumbo jumbo. Where did you find it?"

"My friend Charlotte found it. In a book. What's the Wheel of Fortune?"

"It's a very open-ended kind of card," said Aunt Marina, handing it back to Lauren. "It might signify that your fortune is going to turn."

"Like, the person might have bad luck or something?"

"Not necessarily. It may go up, or it may go down. It generally means there might be a change in a person's life, for better or worse."

Lauren nodded. She stuck the card back in her bag. It's not like she believed this stuff or anything, but still. It was a relief to know it wasn't necessarily a bad omen.

"Thanks, Aunt Marina," said Lauren. "I better get going. Lots of homework."

"Want me to drive you?"

"No, it's not raining anymore. I'm good." She gave Aunt Marina a hug and was on her way.

As she walked toward home, she pulled out her phone to text Charlotte.

Aunt Marina says the card is no big deal. It's the Wheel of Fortune. It just means your luck may go up or down.

Almost immediately Charlotte texted her back.

Oh, good. Thanks. BTW what's the math homework again?

Lauren grinned. Charlotte never seemed to remember her planner. As she reached the corner, she swiveled her backpack around and clenched it to her side in order to unzip it and pull out her planner. She stepped down off the curb.

"Watch out!"

Her reflexes reacted before her brain did. She leaped backward, stumbling and almost falling, just in the nick of time before a bicyclist zoomed past her. It was a delivery guy.

"Watch where you're going!" he yelled over his shoulder, and disappeared around the next corner.

Lauren's heart was thudding. That was a close call. She texted the math pages to Charlotte. Then she added,

Oh by the way, thanks to you, I almost got run down by a delivery guy on a bike.

What??

JK LOL. I just stepped off the curb without looking. Must remind self. No more texting while walking.

Charlotte texted back.

Be careful!

But that night another terrible thing happened to Lauren, and this time there was nothing she could do to stop it. She had a nightmare that spiders were crawling all over her.

CHAPTER 7

The next morning, just as Lauren had settled into her seat on the bus, Stacy plunked herself down into the empty seat next to her.

"Got the lab?" she asked, without bothering to say hello.

With a sigh, Lauren pulled out her notebook and handed it to Stacy. "You realize this is blackmail, right?" she said.

Stacy smiled sweetly, her pink lip gloss sparkling in the morning sun. "I prefer to think of it as a mutually beneficial arrangement." She moved back to the back of the bus again, leaving Lauren alone, seething quietly.

Lauren and Charlotte had gym together, second period.

"So, yeah. Aunt Marina says the card is nothing to worry about," said Lauren as she and Charlotte sat side by side on the bench, tying their sneakers.

"I know this is going to sound silly, but that's reassuring in a weird way," said Charlotte. "I'm not, like, superstitious or anything, but with my dad away and all, I just don't need any bad luck right now."

Lauren smiled. She didn't say anything about the terrible dream she'd had last night. Why worry Charlotte? "Yeah, it's silly to be superstitious," agreed Lauren. "This is like feeling guilty about breaking a chain e-mail. I always delete those things right away."

"Me too," said Charlotte, although from the way Charlotte looked away quickly, Lauren wasn't sure if she was being completely truthful.

"You want the card back, or should I just toss it?" asked Lauren.

"I guess you can give it back," said Charlotte. "It's kind of cool-looking. I can use it as a bookmark."

Lauren rummaged around in her bag. "Huh. That's funny. It's not in here. Sorry, I guess I must have lost it."

"No big deal," said Charlotte, standing up.

"Let's move along, ladies!" called Ms. Behr, poking

her head into the locker room. "We're starting basket-ball today!"

Charlotte and Lauren both groaned.

Stacy came dashing into the locker room seconds after the second bell had rung. "Sorry, Ms. Behr!" she called. "I was helping Ms. Monti make a collection for the clothing drive and lost track of time!"

Ms. Behr frowned at Stacy. "You know how I feel about liars. Now hustle up and join us in the gym when you are ready." She left the locker room.

Stacy's mouth gaped open like a fish. "What's with her today?" she asked her friends, who were waiting for her to change. "She always buys my lame excuses. Every teacher does."

Ava shook her head. "All the teachers love you," she said. "Who knows why the old bear's growling today."

Charlotte and Lauren looked at each other and smiled just a little. It was nice to see Stacy admonished in front of everyone. A change from the way teachers usually fawned all over her.

"All right, everyone! We'll start with the fundamentals," called Ms. Behr when the girls were all assembled in the gym. "First a free throw contest! Form teams of four! Keep track of your shots! The team with the fewest free throws runs two laps!"

Charlotte and Lauren teamed up with Gwen and Allie, who were also terrible basketball players. Stacy, Maddy, Katie, and Ava immediately formed a team. They were the best athletes in the grade.

"Wow, you guys," said Gwen to Charlotte and Lauren after they'd each taken their turn. "When did you both become such good shooters? You each made eight out of ten shots!"

Charlotte laughed. "Beginner's luck?"

Lauren shook her head. "No idea."

Lauren and Charlotte's team came in second place. Stacy's team came in last.

"I thought they were all good basketball players," Charlotte murmured to Lauren, as the rest of the class watched Stacy's team run two laps. Stacy glowered at them as she passed by.

Lauren shrugged. "I thought so too. Maybe Stacy's having a little bad luck today. And from the looks she keeps giving us, you'd think it was all *our* fault."

"Here's your notebook back," said Stacy to Lauren after lunch that day. The second bell hadn't yet rung as kids filed into science.

Lauren took the notebook and then did a double take, staring at Stacy's face. "What happened?" asked Lauren.

"Thanks for pointing it out," Stacy said sarcastically. "If you must know, I seem to have had an allergic reaction to something. It must have started during gym class, because why else would I miss so many shots?" With a toss of her head, she continued to her desk.

Ms. Monti was writing the lab partners on the board. With a combination of thrill and horror, Lauren saw that she was paired with Peter Clark. She'd had a secret crush on him since the first day of school. Along with every other seventh-grade girl. She could feel Stacy glaring at her from a few desks away, but she refused to look.

Lauren and Peter sat down next to each other.

"I hear you're a science whiz," said Peter, nudging her with his elbow.

Lauren could feel herself blushing. "Well, my dad's a scientist so I guess it rubbed off a little or whatever." She smiled at him.

Zing!

A rubber band flew off her braces and hit Stacy, two lab tables away, in the arm.

Lauren's face immediately flushed. She tried to die of embarrassment right on the spot, but couldn't.

Stacy whirled around to see what had hit her arm. She saw Lauren staring at her and their eyes locked. Lauren looked away quickly, only to see Peter staring at her from the other direction, a look of disgust and amusement on his face.

Ms. Monti clapped her hands to get their attention. "For today's lab, each group needs to transfer fruit flies *carefully* into their own vial. Watch me, so you learn how."

The class watched her take the vial full of fruit flies and tap it gently on the counter. Then she quickly removed the foam stopper on the vial, placed a new vial over the old one, turned it upside down, and gently tapped a few flies into the new one before recapping both vials. "Do it carefully now," she cautioned.

Two by two, teams of lab partners tapped out their own supply of fruit flies and then passed the vial filled with fruit flies to the next pair.

"You want to try it?" Peter said to Lauren, after Stacy

had passed them the vial teeming with the tiny fruit flies. "I'm nervous about making the transfer."

"It's easy," scoffed Lauren. "I've done it loads of times at my dad's lab." She picked up the vial. "See, you just move it over the other vial and tap it like this, and then—"

Several flies suddenly flew toward her face, startling her. "Oh!" she said, and dropped the vial on the counter. She had thought the connection she'd made between the vial was secure. So how could flies have escaped from it?

The vial rolled off the desk and bounced onto the floor, dislodging the cap at the other end as well.

A swarm of fruit flies rose up in a small, dark cloud as they all escaped from both ends of the vial and zoomed around the classroom.

Several girls screamed. Lots of people ducked for cover under their lab desks. Even Ms. Monti looked dismayed as she picked up a set of papers she'd been grading to whap away at the swarm of flies.

"Open the window!" she called. "Try to fan them in that direction!"

And chaos ensued for the next several minutes.

CHAPTER 8

"I heard about science," said Charlotte, as she and Lauren stood side by side at their lockers between social studies and last period. "Sounds rough."

Lauren groaned. "How did you hear so fast?"

"News like that travels fast. And besides, there seem to be flies all over the school. I saw one bobbing around in the library."

"I have no idea how that happened. I just wasn't expecting any flies, and then they flew in my face and I guess it startled me so much I—" She groaned again. "And in front of Peter Clark, too!"

A fruit fly flew lazily past them, then continued down the hallway.

Charlotte suppressed a grin. Poor Lauren. She would never live this one down. They'd be calling her Fruit Fly until high school graduation.

"Not one of my better moments," said Lauren, shoving a notebook into her locker and rummaging around for her Spanish book. "It was—hey! Look. Here's that tarot card of yours I thought I lost. I guess it must have been shoved inside my science notebook all day, the one that I loaned to Stacy. Still want it?"

Charlotte shrugged. "Sure. I guess so." She took the card from Lauren and stuck it into her own bag.

Stacy walked by with Ava and Maddy. "Great going in science today, Laur-Laur," she said in a singsongy voice. "Good thing it wasn't a spider lab."

Ava and Maddy both cracked up.

"Thanks, Stacy," said Lauren drily. "Appreciate your sympathy."

"Next time, be more careful and make sure the cap on the bottom of the vial is fully on. Always good to check," said Stacy over her shoulder, and the three girls continued on their way.

"You don't think—," said Charlotte.

"I wonder—," said Lauren.

They'd both spoken at the same time. They both looked at each other.

"Do you think Stacy rigged the vial like that on purpose?" asked Lauren, staring at Charlotte in disbelief. "Of course the stopper could have come free from the force of the fall from the table to the floor, but it seemed to pop off so easily, and that's why so many fruit flies escaped. Stacy's the one who handed it to me. Maybe she fixed it so it looked like the stopper was in, but maybe it really wasn't."

Charlotte blinked at her. "Why would she do that?"

Lauren shrugged. "No clue. She's already blackmailing me for my notes." She told Charlotte about the compromising video Stacy had taken on the bus.

"It's hard to know for sure, I guess," said Charlotte.

Lauren shook her head slowly back and forth. "I guess I've had quite a bit of bad luck today." She told Charlotte about the rubber band flying off her braces and hitting Stacy. "That was bad enough, but did it have to happen in front of Peter Clark?" Lauren's face got hot with humiliation just thinking about it.

Charlotte shook her head and patted her friend's shoulder sympathetically. But there was an uneasy feeling beginning to creep and crawl through her thoughts.

When she got home that afternoon, the twins were still furious with Charlotte about the pink uniforms. Their mom had put them through the wash twice that day, with several different kinds of bleaching detergents, and they were slightly better, but you could still see the pink tint.

"The guys are calling us Pink One and Pink Two," said Jon, when Charlotte walked in Wednesday afternoon.

"Even the other team was laughing at us," said Tom.

Charlotte apologized to them again. "I'm really sorry, guys," she said.

That night, as Charlotte was in her room doing her homework, she got a text. The number was unfamiliar. She opened it up.

I told you to pass the card along. Do it, or darkness will descend on you.

Her entire body jolted as though it had been shocked. She pressed her glasses more closely toward the bridge of her nose and stared at the text. Should she ignore it? Was it someone at school playing a joke on her? But who knew about the card?

Her mind began rapidly calculating. Lauren, of course, knew about the card. But she would never play a mean trick like this. Would she? Who else knew about it? Stacy had seen the card during homeroom yesterday. But she would have no way of knowing about the message written across the back. Lauren's Aunt Marina? Impossible and ridiculous.

Charlotte studied the phone number attached to the text. It had thirteen digits. Was that some kind of mistake? Phone numbers usually had ten digits, not thirteen. She went over to her computer and plugged the sequence into a search engine, hoping that it would reveal the phone number's owner. But nothing came up that would indicate that this was even a phone number, let alone who it belonged to.

Charlotte called Lauren. She answered right away.

"What's up, Char? Found a fruit fly in your backpack and calling to complain? You'll have to wait your turn."

"No, I . . ." Charlotte hesitated.

"What's the matter? You okay?"

"I'm fine. Did you just send me a text by any chance?"

"Me? No. Why?"

"I just got a weird text. From a weird number. It was

about the card. I just wondered."

"Are you still freaking out about the dumb card, Charlotte? I never had you pegged as a superstitious type. Why don't you just toss it if it's freaking you out so much?"

"I don't think I should," said Charlotte. "I mean, I can't really explain why. I know it's silly of me. Is it silly?"

"Yeah," Lauren replied bluntly. "The card was probably inside that old book for ages. Whoever wrote that message on the back of it is probably an old person. They might even be dead by now."

Charlotte drew in her breath in alarm.

"Okay, wrong thing to say. My point is, there's no way the person who wrote that on the card could also be texting you. Someone you know must be messing around with you."

"I guess you're right," said Charlotte uncertainly.

"Listen, if it will make you feel better, you can give the card to me, okay? Then I will throw it away and accept the consequences. I'm the daughter of a scientist, so it's in my DNA—I don't have a superstitious cell in my body. Since I don't believe in this stuff, it will have no effect on me. Sound good?"

Relief washed over Charlotte. "Okay, thanks. If you are sure you don't mind."

"I definitely don't mind," said Lauren. "Now I have to get going. My dad is trying to reheat something in the microwave, and I have to make sure he doesn't blow up the kitchen."

Charlotte tossed and turned much of that night. Who was it that had sent that text? Who else knew about it? Could Stacy have somehow sent it? Charlotte was thinking back to the events of the previous day when suddenly she jolted upright.

Stacy had been in possession of the card yesterday. Lauren had told her about Stacy borrowing her science notebook. Charlotte flashed back to when Lauren had found the card she'd thought she'd lost. It had been inside her science notebook. The one Stacy had borrowed.

She remembered how Stacy had showed up late for gym. How she had missed so many free throws. How she'd had an allergic reaction to something at lunchtime. Was all that bad luck because she'd had the card with her?

I really am acting silly, she thought. This is anxiety stuff. Charlotte often got this way. She was a middle-of-the-night worrier. Almost always, when she'd fretted about something, she would wake up in the morning and realize how silly she'd been. But right now, Charlotte couldn't ignore the ominous thoughts. The card was a jinx. The person who wrote the message on the back cursed it so it brought bad luck to whoever had it. Should she really pass the card to Lauren, now that she was growing increasingly certain that it brought bad luck? What had Lauren's aunt said? Maybe the Wheel of Fortune card just changed a person's luck. Maybe if that person were having bad luck, and came into possession of the card, the person's luck might change to good luck.

Maybe she was simply rationalizing the problem away. After all, most Wheel of Fortune cards probably didn't have some crazy message scrawled on them by who knows who.

The next morning, when she woke up, Charlotte felt much less anxious about the card. She was certain she was just being silly. If Lauren didn't care, neither did she.

Her mother was sitting glassy eyed at the kitchen table when Charlotte emerged for breakfast. Her eyes were puffy, as though she'd been crying.

"What's wrong, Mom?" Charlotte asked quickly,

barely daring to breathe. "Is Daddy okay? Did you hear something?"

Charlotte's mom closed her eyes and drew a long breath in. Then she let it out quickly. "He's fine, honey. I heard from him late last night, after you were asleep. He's fine, but he's not coming home as early as we thought. It looks like it might be another—" She swallowed, gathered herself. "Another two months."

Charlotte sat down heavily in a chair, absorbing the horror of this news. Then her mind turned to the card. Maybe all that middle-of-the-night anxiety hadn't been so silly. Maybe the card really was doing this. It had to be. It brought bad luck to whoever had it.

Well, Lauren had *agreed to take it,* she thought. Time to pass it along . . . for good.

CHAPTER 9

That day at lunch, Charlotte slid the card across the table to Lauren. There hadn't been any time in homeroom, and they didn't want Stacy anywhere near them when they did the exchange.

"What's that?" asked Gwen, who was sitting next to Lauren.

"Nothing," both girls replied at almost exactly the same time.

Gwen glanced at the card, shrugged, and went back to chatting with Cassie on her other side.

"Are you sure about this?" Charlotte spoke to Lauren in a low voice, just loud enough for Lauren to be able to hear over the din in the cafeteria. "I don't want anything bad to happen to you."

"Stop being a dork," scoffed Lauren, picking up the card and shoving it into her backpack. "The card is nothing. Okay?" Lauren reached across the table and broke off a piece of Charlotte's cookie. "Anyway, if you really—" She coughed. Then she coughed again. Her face turned pink.

"Laur? You okay?" asked Charlotte, springing out of her chair.

Lauren was now coughing harder. Gwen wheeled around and banged Lauren on the back. Lauren grabbed her milk and took a big sip.

"I'm fine!" she sputtered. "You can stop whacking me now!"

"Sure you're okay?" asked Gwen worriedly.

"I'm fine. Really. Everyone turn around and go back to what you were doing," said Lauren through gritted teeth. "I'm already trying to live down the fruit fly thing. I don't need the whole school watching you perform the Heimlich maneuver on me."

Gwen laughed and turned back to Cassie.

Charlotte sat back down, still regarding her friend warily.

"I'm okay, really," said Lauren, slightly irritably. "I just breathed in a piece of cookie is all."

At play rehearsal that afternoon Lauren delivered the wrong line at the wrong place, causing them to have to skip a whole scene.

"Lauren," said Mr. Thompson, the director. "Please don't do that again. All right, start from the top of scene three, everyone." He massaged his temples as though his head was throbbing.

After rehearsal, as Lauren was hurrying to catch the late bus, she got her necklace hooked to her locker, and when she closed the door, it exploded into an avalanche of bouncing beads. By the time she'd collected most of them, she'd missed the bus home from school.

She texted her father at work.

**Missed the bus. Walking home.
Everything fine. I'll walk Teddy. See you
at dinner?**

There was no immediate answer from her dad, so she started walking home. It was a beautiful September afternoon, and the warm, late-summer sun cast a golden light on the trees and the sidewalk. *Really,* she thought, *I ought to walk home more often. Except that poor Teddy will be anxiously waiting for me when I get home.*

A minute or so later her phone buzzed. She flicked it on, assuming it was her dad. But it was from an unknown number—a number with thirteen digits.

You should not have taken the card.
Fear for yourself. And for your dog.

She stopped dead in the middle of the sidewalk, staring at the text. An elderly lady pushing a shopping cart rammed into her from behind.

"Watch what you're doing, young lady!" she barked at Lauren, muttering about newfangled gizmos as she continued on her way.

"Sorry!" Lauren said absently. She looked again at the text. It couldn't possibly be from Charlotte. But who else knew about the card? Hadn't Charlotte mentioned that she, Charlotte, had gotten a weird text? This was a little odd, she was forced to admit. Could it be Stacy? Stacy didn't even have Lauren's phone number. Still, she could have easily gotten it from someone.

Threatening her was bad enough. But threatening her dog?

A feeling of dread passed over her. It was too much of a coincidence that she'd just texted her dad about Teddy and that someone had then threatened to hurt him. Was someone somehow hacking into her phone? What an awful thought. It was probably just some annoying kid being a jerk, but still.

Teddy.

She broke into a run. By the time she got home, she was completely out of breath and half-hysterical with worry.

"Teddy? Teddy!" she bellowed, throwing open the side door and practically falling inside.

For a second all was quiet. And then she heard a thump above her and the jingle of a collar. Teddy came padding down the steps, tail wagging, tongue out.

"Hey, buddy," she said, stooping down and letting him nuzzle her all over her face, her head, her neck. She threw her arms around his neck. "You're okay, aren't you, boy? Of course you are." She stood up and grabbed his leash off the hook. "Come on. We'll go for a walk."

As they headed out the door, Lauren paused a

minute. She stepped back inside and fished through her backpack until she found the card.

"I still don't believe it," she said out loud. Teddy looked up at her and cocked his head to one side, as though trying to understand her. "But why take unnecessary risks? Let's get rid of this." As they headed down the path, she tossed the card into the outside garbage can.

Later, as Lauren was putting a pot of water on the stove for pasta, she got a call from Charlotte.

"Is everything okay?" asked Charlotte anxiously.

"Of course," said Lauren, putting a lid on the pot and turning on the gas. "Why wouldn't it be?"

"Um, no reason," said Charlotte.

"Are you still worried about that dumb card?" asked Lauren.

"Okay, yeah, a little."

"Well, no need to worry," said Lauren. "I chucked it."

Charlotte was quiet for a moment. "Okay. I guess. I hope that's the end of it."

Lauren heard her dad's key in the lock. "Dad's home. Gotta go," she said, and they hung up.

"Hey, Laur!" said her dad, plunking down his heavy shoulder bag and stepping over to give Lauren a big hug. He had dark circles under his eyes, as though he hadn't slept well in days. "What's for dinner? I'm starved. I think I forgot to eat lunch today."

Lauren smiled and rolled her eyes. "It's a good thing you have me around to remind you to eat and sleep. It's spaghetti from a box and sauce from a jar. My specialty."

"School go okay today?" he said, moving over to the stove and opening the lid on the spaghetti sauce.

"Yeah, it was good. I kind of whiffed in rehearsal, though. Skipped a whole scene."

"That's nice, honey," said her dad, who obviously hadn't heard a word she said. Lauren shook her head. She was used to her dad's forgetfulness. He was always thinking about his work, or his classes, or—

Suddenly they heard a yelp.

"Teddy?" they both said at the same time. They rushed into the other room.

"Teddy!" shrieked Lauren, flying over to where the little dog was standing next to the couch. He whimpered and tried to walk toward her, his little stumpy tail wagging feebly, but his front paw was curled under awkwardly.

Her dad had also rushed over, and he crouched at Lauren's side, examining Teddy. He picked him up gently. "Looks like he might have broken his leg," he said grimly. "Get me a couch cushion, a small one."

Lauren grabbed a cushion and handed it to her father, her eyes wide with horror.

"Probably landed funny when he jumped off the couch," said her dad. "Turn off the stuff on the stove, okay? Then find my keys and my wallet. I think they're in my jacket pocket. You can call Dr. Stone from the car and let him know we're on our way."

Two hours later, Lauren and her dad were heading home from the vet. Teddy lay on the cushion in Lauren's lap, apparently still woozy from his procedure. His front right leg had been shaved of all its fur well past his elbow, and his lower paw was encased in a bright red cast. She stroked him gently.

"Poor little guy," said her dad, reaching out a hand to pet the little dog. "Such a freak accident, too. He's jumped off that couch about a thousand times. Guess this was just an unlucky day for him."

Lauren was lost in thought. She was thinking about the card. She was thinking about the text she'd gotten. How it had threatened her dog. She couldn't believe she was thinking this, but it couldn't be just a coincidence. It's not as though someone could have been in the house and pushed him off the couch. Of course it could all just be nothing more than random bad luck. But still. She was thinking that maybe the change in fortune Aunt Marina had talked about wasn't just a bunch of superstitious nonsense after all.

Later, after they'd finally had their dinner and her dad had retired to his office to grade papers, Lauren slipped outside with a flashlight. She opened the lid to the trash can and shined the light inside. Luckily, the card was sitting right on top and she didn't have to do any digging through the trash.

She fished it out and put it into her pocket. Then she tiptoed back inside.

Upstairs in her room she studied the card under the light of her reading lamp. She turned it over, reading and rereading the message scrawled across the back. It looked as though it had been written so very long ago. The ink was faded and scratched in some places.

She thought about the threatening text she'd gotten. There was no way the texter was the same person that had written this message on the back of the card. That texter *had* to have been some kid hacking her phone, and Teddy's accident was just bad luck. Because no one pushed Teddy off the couch.

And yet, Lauren couldn't deny it. Despite her logical and analytical mind she could not deny that this card really did seem to bring the bearer bad luck. It was too much of a coincidence that when she'd gotten the card back from Charlotte at lunch, she'd almost immediately choked on a bite of cookie. And then she'd skipped a scene at play practice. And broken her necklace. And missed the bus. And—poor Teddy. She shivered. Then she sat, lost in thought, for quite some time.

By the time she was ready for bed, she'd come to a decision. She was going to slip the card into Charlotte's backpack the next day, without Charlotte knowing. After all, it was Charlotte's card.

CHAPTER 10

The next day in science, Charlotte's teacher, Mr. Madden, walked around the classroom, passing back tests. He placed Charlotte's gently on the desk in front of her, face down. Charlotte didn't like the look he gave her. Somewhere between bewilderment and disappointment.

Slowly she turned it over. A seventy-six? On a *science* test? She quickly put it back down on the desk, her ears burning, her mouth dry. This was the worst grade she'd gotten, possibly ever. She turned it back over and looked at it quickly. Oh. She had switched around the formulas for weight and acceleration. How could she have done something like that?

At lunch Charlotte was heading toward her table

carrying her lunch tray, her heavy backpack on her back, when her right foot stepped on a slippery patch on the floor. Her foot slid forward, causing her to lose her balance and fall backward.

Crash!

Applause.

Humiliation, as a teacher and a girl she didn't know helped her to her feet and began picking up the spilled contents of her tray.

Lauren and Gwen and Cassie and several others from her lunch table helped get her another lunch and were really nice about it of course, but Charlotte noticed that Lauren had a weird look on her face. An anxious look.

There were no further mishaps that afternoon, until English class, which was the last period of the day. During the second half of class they watched part of the film of *A Midsummer Night's Dream*. Ms. Zarchin paused the film at the end of act 2, and turned on the lights.

"We can watch more on Monday," she said. "Charlotte, would you mind bringing the DVD back to the library? The bell's going to ring in a few minutes, so you had better pack up your things so you can head directly out to your bus after that."

Charlotte packed up and took the DVD from Ms. Zarchin.

The library was on the first floor, but her English class was at the end of a very long wing, so it was a good hike from her classroom. The bell hadn't yet rung, and the hallways were still empty.

Mrs. Barber, the school librarian, was just putting on her sweater when Charlotte came in. "Oh, hello, Charlotte," she said. "I'm on bus duty this afternoon. What do you need?"

"Just returning the DVD," said Charlotte.

"Lovely." She took the DVD and scanned it into the system, and then handed it back to Charlotte. "Can you put it in the AV room on the 'To be Reshelved' cart? I'm late already. Then be sure to lock the door when you leave—DVDs have a way of walking off!"

Charlotte promised she would, and Mrs. Barber hurried away.

The light switch was outside the room. Charlotte flicked it on and walked in, threading her way through carts of projectors and televisions toward the back wall, where the DVDs were kept. She'd just set the DVD on the cart when her phone buzzed. It was a text.

I told you to pass it on.

Her stomach dropped and a bolt of fear shot through her. She was still staring at the text on her phone when the door suddenly swung closed. Then the light went out.

"Hey!" yelled Charlotte, moving toward the door and immediately bashing her hip against a rolling cart. "Ow! Hey! I'm in here!" Her voice came out thin and high and panicky.

Whoever had closed the door either didn't hear her, or ignored her.

It was pitch-dark. Like black construction paper. No light whatsoever.

"Don't panic," Charlotte muttered to herself, but already she could feel her heart racing, her palms sweating. "Just get to the door. Open the door. Everything will be fine."

Then she remembered her cell phone. She could use it as a flashlight! With trembling hands she clicked it on. A dim but usable light emanated from its screen, allowing her to see her path to the door. She held it up with a shaky hand, so it could illuminate her way.

And promptly dropped the phone.

She heard it clatter and skitter across the floor. Its dim light vanished, and now she was back in the dark. She dropped to her hands and knees, still wearing her heavy backpack, which shifted around and almost made her fall over. She readjusted it and then felt around, patting every inch of the floor in search of the phone. Her breathing was shallow, her heart pounding in her ears. She tried not to think of that day, so many years ago, when she'd felt the hand on her shoulder. But of course, she did think of it. Why did her mind go directly to the memories she most wanted to forget? Like when you have a sore inside your mouth and your tongue insists on prodding that sore place.

Her hand closed around the phone. With a surge of relief, she clicked it on.

Nothing happened.

Had she broken it when she'd dropped it? That ruled out any possibility of calling someone to come rescue her. But that was silly anyway. All she had to do was get to the door without having a full-blown panic attack.

She kept moving forward on hands and knees, negotiating her way around rolling carts and tangles of heavy wires. And then she could see light shining underneath the heavy door.

She stood up, moved toward the door, and felt where the doorknob was.

It didn't budge.

She was locked in.

A new wave of panic surged through her, all the way down to her toes. She pounded on the door with the heel of her hand.

"Help!" she yelled. "Someone let me out of here! Hello? Anyone there?"

The janitor must have come by and locked up, she reasoned. What if she was here all night? What if Mrs. Barber didn't return to the library after her bus duty? What if this room was completely soundproof? Then she remembered it was Friday. What if she was stuck here all weekend?

She pounded harder, trying not to cry.

"Someone! Help!" More pounding. Rattling of the knob. "I'm locked in here! Help! Hello?"

More pounding. More frantic rattling. The lump in

her throat felt like a golf ball. Her pulse was racing. She pounded until her hands went numb, expecting at any second to feel the hand on her shoulder.

And that's when she could have sworn she felt something brush through her hair. Fingers? Spiders?

She yelled for another half a minute, although in her terror it felt like hours.

And then she heard the doorknob turn. The door swung open.

She slung herself out of the door and into the library, blinking at the sudden brightness, and bent over and shook her hair out. Thankfully there were no bugs in it, although that begged the question of what had brushed through it.

She righted herself and scanned the room. There was no one in the library. How had the door come unlocked? She turned and looked at the lock. The doorknob could only be locked or unlocked with a key. Could it have come unstuck somehow, when she'd been rattling the knob?

It seemed unlikely. Something very strange and very scary was going on.

Outside the library windows she could see just a few

stragglers rushing by, heading for their buses. She hadn't been in the closet very long. Should she try to make her bus? The clock told her it was too late. She'd never make it. Anyway, maybe it was better to walk home. It might calm her down.

Then she remembered the text she'd gotten. She pulled out her phone and clicked the power button.

Now her phone was working again.

She checked the mysterious text. Why would the texter think she still had the card? She'd given it to Lauren. And Lauren had thrown it out.

She thought back to the way Lauren had behaved at lunch today. She'd been almost more upset about Charlotte dropping her tray than Charlotte had been. And her whole demeanor had been odd. Not really looking her in the eye. Furtive darting eyes. A thought struck Charlotte.

"Could Lauren have slipped it back to me?" she asked herself out loud. She set her backpack down on a library table and began rummaging through it.

In the outside pocket her fingers closed on a thick piece of cardboard. She drew out the card.

"I can't believe it," she whispered, staring at the card

in horror. "After all that talk about not being superstitious. Not believing all the mumbo jumbo. And then she passed it back to me. Without telling me."

Her phone vibrated on the table. Almost afraid to look, she picked it up and checked the text.

Pass it along or your dad won't be coming home.

Charlotte walked home slowly, lost in thought, on the verge of tears. Her best friend had treacherously slipped the card into her backpack, and now she'd gotten the scariest text message she could imagine and she was terrified for her dad. The question now was, what to do next? What would she do with this stupid card? Could she bring herself to pass it along to some unsuspecting person, just to get it out of her possession? She thought about Stacy. Stacy would be the perfect person to pass the card along to. She was so mean. She almost deserved bad luck.

Charlotte stopped in her tracks. What was she thinking? She was horrified with herself. She couldn't do that. She couldn't intentionally bring bad luck to someone, even someone she didn't like. But she had to do something before the worst happened. She resumed walking, even more slowly than before.

She heard footsteps approaching. Running footsteps. She turned around and was surprised to see Lauren nearly upon her, her long legs moving with surprising speed, her backpack bouncing on her shoulders. She skidded to a stop in front of Charlotte.

"Char," she panted, doubling over and putting her hands on her knees, trying to catch her breath. "I—I— have to tell you something."

"I already know," said Charlotte coldly. "You gave it back to me. I just found it."

"I'm so sorry!" cried Lauren, standing back up and looking at her friend pleadingly. "I didn't want to do it. I feel awful about it. I just sort of panicked. After all that stuff I said about not believing in it. And then all these terrible things started happening to me, and then Teddy got hurt last night. He broke his leg!"

Charlotte's eyes widened in horror.

"I know it was wrong of me to pass it back to you! I'll take it back. Figure something out."

Charlotte's anger toward Lauren vanished. After all,

she had done almost the same thing to Lauren—she'd given her the card when she'd been almost positive that it really and truly did bring bad luck to the holder. Who was she to judge Lauren for coming to the same conclusion?

"It's okay, Laur," she said. "I get it. I know. I'm not going to give it back to you. I have to figure out what to do. I'm the one who found it. I'm the one who has to deal with it."

"So you don't think it's a coincidence anymore either?" asked Lauren, looking worried.

"I'm convinced that it's not," said Charlotte. "There are too many coincidences for it to be a coincidence. Do you know what I mean?"

Lauren nodded.

"Do you have time to sit?" Charlotte asked. "Maybe it'd help to write everything down." She gestured toward a small park off the main street, which had several empty benches.

"Good idea," said Lauren. "We'll make a list."

When the girls were sitting side by side, Charlotte pulled out her notebook. "First, tell me all the bad things that happened to you when you had the card in your possession."

"Teddy breaking his leg," said Lauren promptly.

Charlotte wrote that down. "Poor Teddy," she murmured. "Now what else. Didn't you say your dad got a speeding ticket?"

"Yes, and that messed up all kinds of stuff for him about getting his grant. And then remember how I told you I got knocked down by that guy texting? And then how I almost got run over by that delivery guy in the road?" Lauren was ticking off the episodes on her finger.

"You left your planner at school, remember?" said Charlotte. "You never do that."

Lauren nodded. "And the fruit flies." She buried her face in her hands, remembering that episode. "And me hitting Stacy with the rubber band from my braces." Her words were now tumbling out in a rush. "And skipping a whole scene in rehearsal. And breaking my necklace, which made me miss the late bus, which made me late getting home." She stared at Charlotte. "All little stuff, really. But there's *lots* of little stuff."

Charlotte nodded grimly and finished scribbling it all down. "Now me," she said. "My dad. My dad found out he isn't allowed to come home yet, even though he was supposed to."

Lauren nodded. "That's the worst one. Are there other things though?"

"I've been having bad dreams."

Lauren's eyes widened. "Me too!"

"And remember how I told you I turned the twins' uniforms pink?"

"That happened when you first had the card, didn't it?" mused Lauren, thinking back.

Charlotte nodded. She wrote that down, then chewed the end of her pencil eraser, thinking. "I got a bad grade on my science test. I dropped my tray at lunch. And just a little while ago, I got locked into the AV room." She shuddered. "The door closed by itself, I swear. I was jiggling the doorknob frantically and screaming for help. And then the door just opened. I thought someone was playing a trick on me, that they'd locked me in on purpose, but there was no one in the library when the door opened."

Lauren looked at her, her eyes round with horror.

"And I had a very weird episode in the woods behind the library on Monday." She told Lauren about the whispering she'd heard. "And the freakiest thing of all? I'm getting texts from someone. Someone I don't know."

"Me too!" said Lauren. "I thought it might be Stacy."

"That's what I thought too," said Charlotte. "But now I don't think so." She held back tears as she showed Lauren the most recent text she'd received. She felt nauseous with anxiety.

The two girls sat side by side, staring around the deserted little park. It had a small playground for little kids, but the sun was beginning to set, and the temperature had dropped rapidly. It was too cold and windy for anyone to be out there now. A pigeon flew down from a low window ledge. It strut-walked for a few paces, its head bobbing up and down with each step, and then flew off again.

Lauren turned slowly to Charlotte. "I just realized Stacy must have had the card for a while when she borrowed my notebook to copy off me."

"I know," said Charlotte. "I thought about that, too. While she had the card, she had bad luck. She was late for gym. And then she missed all those shots in basketball."

"And then she had an allergic reaction to something and broke out in spots."

Charlotte banged her notebook against her knees, still gripping it hard with white-knuckled hands. "Laur, what are we going to do?" she said, her voice climbing. "I can't keep this card. You tried throwing it away and that didn't work. But I can't pass it to someone else. Not even my worst enemy!" Her eyes welled up with tears. "I'm worried. About my dad. About what might happen to him if I keep this stupid thing."

"Maybe we can find a really, really sick person to give it to," said Lauren. "Like someone about to die in a hospital."

Charlotte crossed her arms and blinked at her.

"Bad idea. I'm sorry. I don't know what I was thinking. I just feel so desperate."

They sat in silence again. Suddenly Lauren clutched Charlotte's arm excitedly. "I think I just had an idea. One that might actually work and not hurt anyone."

Charlotte looked at her questioningly. She waited.

"My aunt Marina. Duh! Why didn't it occur to me before? I bet she can tell us what to do. She's really knowledgeable about all this stuff. She practically does it for a living!"

"I thought she was an acupuncturist."

"She is. But she knows how to read fortunes. She knows what all the tarot cards mean. When I was little, she used to read my palm and do this thing with tea leaves. I think my uncle Jack was amused by the whole thing, but he never said anything."

Charlotte nodded. "I think that's a good idea, to ask your aunt. And you think she'd believe us?"

"I definitely think so. And maybe she'd know something about getting rid of a curse. I think she'd be happy to be asked. Let me text her and ask if we can go over there tonight. Maybe we can even make it a sleepover."

"You do realize what day it is."

"Friday?" said Lauren.

"Friday the thirteenth," said Charlotte. "Not that I'm superstitious or anything."

"Me neither," said Lauren.

Neither girl could look the other in the eye. They stood up and began walking again.

"Maybe it's a good thing," said Lauren after they'd walked in silence for a while.

"*What's* a good thing?"

"The fact that it's Friday the thirteenth. Maybe we're meant to try something like this on a day like this."

"Maybe you're right," said Charlotte thoughtfully. "But I'm still scared. About what might happen."

"Me too. I'll let you know timing and stuff as soon as

I hear from my aunt," said Lauren as they approached an intersection. Charlotte lived to the right, Lauren to the left.

"Sounds good," said Charlotte.

"Are you mad?"

Charlotte shook her head. "No, of course not."

Lauren blew out a breath of relief. "Just be careful. Remember that stupid card in your backpack. Look both ways and all that."

"I will," said Charlotte.

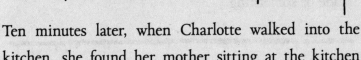

Ten minutes later, when Charlotte walked into the kitchen, she found her mother sitting at the kitchen table, a cup of tea in front of her. She was stirring the tea with a teaspoon and staring into space. She didn't even seem to hear the door, even when Charlotte closed it pretty loudly behind her.

"What's the matter, Mom?" asked Charlotte in a small, frightened voice. "Have you heard something? Something from Dad?"

Her mother looked up at her as though she'd only just realized that Charlotte had walked in. She stood up quickly. "No, no, honey, there's been no news, bad or good. I haven't heard anything. I'm sure he'll be in touch."

Charlotte nodded and opened her arms to hug her mother. Her mother stepped gratefully toward Charlotte and hugged her tightly.

"Is it okay if I go to a sleepover with Lauren tonight at her aunt Marina's house?" asked Charlotte.

Her mother released her from the hug. Her eyes were glinting a little, like they might be wet. "Sure, honey," she said. "I'm off tonight. Maybe I'll take the boys to the arcade or something."

A few minutes later Charlotte's phone buzzed. With shaking hands she looked at the number. Lauren.

It's fine with Aunt Marina for us to sleep over. She's going to make us dinner, too. Meet around 6?

Charlotte texted her back, feeling hugely relieved.

A little while later she shouldered her small overnight bag, kissed her mom, and headed out the door.

Before she'd even made it down the front steps, she got another mysterious text.

Don't go over there tonight. You'll be sorry.

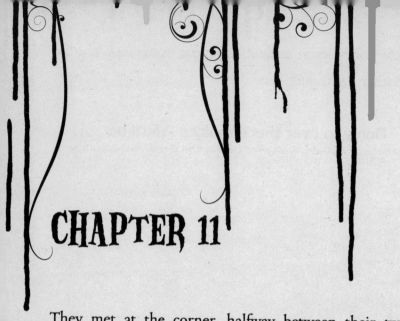

CHAPTER 11

They met at the corner, halfway between their two houses. Charlotte showed Lauren the latest text.

"That settles it. It can't be Stacy who's texting us," said Lauren. "There's no way she could know we were going to my aunt's tonight. Can I look at the other texts?"

Charlotte pulled out her phone and scrolled through her recent messages. She handed Lauren her phone. Lauren handed hers to Charlotte. Each of them read the other's texts.

"Char, I'm scared. This is just too weird. Maybe we should show these to the police or something. They could maybe trace them."

"I thought so too," said Charlotte. "But I have this really funny feeling that they won't be able to find out where they came from. They might not 'come' from anywhere."

"I hope my aunt can help us," said Lauren.

"Me too."

It was a ten minute walk to Aunt Marina's house.

"Is it my imagination, or is the sky getting dark really fast this evening?" asked Charlotte, looking at the dark clouds roiling ominously above the tree line. The full moon was rising, and it looked enormous against the horizon, shrouded in gauzy gray clouds that zoomed past.

"Maybe," said Lauren. "Come on. Let's move faster."

They passed by the library, which was closed up for the night. The beautiful old building looked spooky with no lights on inside. As they walked past the old, gnarled tree in the front of the library, a flock of crows that was roosting in the branches suddenly began chittering, cawing, screeching as the girls passed by.

"Did you hear that?" asked Charlotte, clutching Lauren's arm.

"Hear what? Those crows?"

"No. Not the crows. The whispering! I heard someone whispering my name! Just like I did in the woods."

Lauren shook her head. "I didn't. I was focusing on not getting bird doo on me. Maybe it was the wind. It's gotten really windy out here."

As if to emphasize her words, a sudden gust blew across the sidewalk, sending fallen leaves twirling and dancing in a wild waltz around their ankles.

"Are we almost there?" asked Charlotte.

Lauren pointed. "It's right here."

"I swear I hear someone following us. Can you hear footsteps in the dry leaves? Or am I crazy?" Charlotte asked, the panic barely concealed in her voice.

"I don't hear anything. The next house is Aunt Marina's. Come on. Let's run."

Aunt Marina threw open the door to greet them before they'd even mounted the front steps.

"Hi, Lauren. This must be your friend Charlotte," she said, beaming at Charlotte as she and Lauren hurried up the stairs. "Come on in, girls. It looks like it might rain again. And they're predicting nasty weather for the weekend. Lots of thunderstorms and even a tornado warning. A tornado would certainly be unusual for this time of year."

The girls stepped into her front hallway. Charlotte

felt a huge rush of relief when Aunt Marina closed and locked the door. Inside it was cozy and warm, and there were delicious smells coming from the kitchen.

Aunt Marina wore a zip-up sweatshirt and jeans. She bustled around, showing them where to hang their jackets. "Well, I've cooked a ton of food for us," she said cheerfully. "I made curried vegetables and brown rice, and I even bought organic popcorn for us to eat when we watch a movie tonight!"

Aunt Marina showed Charlotte and Lauren into the guest room, where there were two twin beds made up with colorful quilted bedspreads.

It wasn't until after dinner was over and the dishes were finished that Lauren brought up the card.

"Aunt Marina, remember that card I showed you a few days ago?"

"Of course. The Wheel of Fortune card," said Aunt Marina, setting down her cup of green tea. "Is it giving you trouble?"

Charlotte and Lauren exchanged uneasy looks.

"Well, yeah," said Lauren. "W-we think it's cursed. It brings bad luck."

Taking turns, the girls blurted out the story. The weird

coincidences. The texts. The sort-of awful and truly awful things that had happened to whoever happened to be in possession of the card. Whoever wasn't passing it along.

Aunt Marina listened carefully. She didn't laugh. She didn't scoff. She kept nodding, and then shaking her head with dismay at the bad stuff.

"Do you think we're crazy?" asked Lauren when they'd finally finished.

Aunt Marina shook her head. "No. I don't. When I first saw the card, I thought the message on the back was silly, but after everything you've told me, I believe you're right about the card and its powers. I've heard of such things but never actually seen something like this."

"Is there anything we can do?" asked Charlotte.

"After what we know it can do, we don't want to pass it along to someone," added Lauren. "Even if we put it back in the book and it went to someone we don't know."

Aunt Marina stood up. She tapped a finger thoughtfully against her lips. Then she scooped up Cinders, who'd been sleeping next to her on an empty chair, and began pacing, stroking his head as she did so.

The girls said nothing. It was clear that she was thinking about what to do.

Finally she stopped pacing and turned toward them. "I think I know something we can try to get rid of the curse," she said. "We'll have a ceremony. Tonight."

Charlotte and Lauren exchanged glances. A shudder ran down Charlotte's spine.

Outside, Charlotte realized, it had begun to rain.

"We'll do it here, in the kitchen," said Aunt Marina. "Lauren, find some candles and holders. I'll be back in a few minutes. I just need to consult my references. I've never done anything quite like this before. I guess there's a first time for everything,"

A few minutes later Aunt Marina called the girls into the kitchen. By now the rain was pouring down outside, and Charlotte thought she heard the distant rumble of thunder.

Aunt Marina had changed out of her jeans and sweatshirt. She'd put on a billowy purple blouse over similarly billowy dark silk pants, and she'd taken her hair tie out so that her long blond hair tumbled around her shoulders. She'd spread a red tablecloth over the kitchen table. Three candles, of different heights, flickered in a small cluster at the center. The overhead, recessed lights cast a wan glow over the room. Charlotte smelled something like cinnamon and assumed Aunt Marina was burning incense somewhere, although she couldn't see it.

"Sit," she commanded them.

The girls sat.

No one spoke for a minute. The rain outside and the ticking of the kitchen clock were the only sounds. Charlotte darted a glance at Lauren and met Lauren's gaze. Charlotte felt strangely apprehensive. There was so much at stake. So much depended on Aunt Marina's success. What if she failed?

But Aunt Marina had a look of resolve in her big blue eyes, a confidence that reassured Charlotte.

"We'll start by all closing our eyes," said Aunt Marina in a low, even voice. "We will rid this card of any evil intent."

Lightning illuminated the dim kitchen. Then thunder boomed so loudly that Charlotte and Lauren both jumped. Charlotte opened her eyes a crack to see what was going on. Aunt Marina appeared to be concentrating so hard she seemed not to have heard the thunder. She remained still, her palms face down on the table, the card faceup between her hands, her eyes closed, her brow furrowed with concentration.

Suddenly Aunt Marina's eyes flew open. She stared straight ahead of her. Charlotte had the strangest impression that Aunt Marina was listening to something. Charlotte could hear nothing but the rain and the clock.

Wait. Was there something else? Was the whispering starting?

Charrrrrrrrlooooooooootte.

Lauren had her eyes closed. She didn't seem to have heard. Aunt Marina's eyes were open, and she still looked like she was listening, but maybe she heard something else.

Charrrrrrrrlooooooooootte. Stoooooop herrrrrrrr!

Charlotte gulped.

Aunt Marina nodded, ever so slightly. She turned in her chair and reached for something on the counter behind her, something Charlotte hadn't noticed before. Something bright glinted in Aunt Marina's hand. She turned back to the table, and Charlotte could see that she was holding a large pair of pointed scissors, the kind her mother kept in her sewing box.

Aunt Marina picked up the card. She was murmuring something under her breath, but Charlotte couldn't hear it beneath the steady patter of rain.

Stoooooop herrrrrrrr!

"We must rid this card of any evil intent," Aunt Marina repeated, this time in a louder, clearer voice.

Noooooooooo!

"We must cut its energy in twain." With that, she opened the scissors wide and snipped the card in half.

Charlotte and Lauren both gasped.

Ahhhhhhhhhhhh!

As soon as the two pieces of the card dropped to the table, the lights began to flicker.

"And in twain again," said Aunt Marina, seemingly oblivious to the cries Charlotte had heard, to the blinking lights all around them. She picked up one of the two pieces of card and snipped it in half. Then the other piece.

Lightning flashed. Thunder boomed. The lights flickered one last time and went out. Charlotte's blood felt like ice in her veins. The only light in the kitchen now came from the candles, and they were flickering wildly, as though an unseen breeze was trying to blow them out.

Aunt Marina snipped another piece in half.

The candles went out completely.

Snip. Charlotte could hear the scissors once again.

The candles relit.

Charlotte's hands gripped the edge of the table. Her knuckles quickly turned white.

Snip.

The door to the kitchen blew open, hitting the wall behind it so hard a pane of glass shattered. All the cupboard doors in the kitchen banged open, and Charlotte could hear glasses and cups breaking.

Outside, someone—or something—howled in anguish.

Lauren shrieked.

So she was as scared as Charlotte.

Snip.

Now Charlotte heard a roaring in her ears. Could the others hear it too? It sounded like ten chain saws going in an enclosed tunnel. Deafening. She clutched her ears to drown it out, scrunching her shoulders to ward it away.

How many more snips did Aunt Marina make?

Charlotte didn't know. But suddenly the roaring stopped. The door, eerily, slowly, swung closed, latching gently. Then the electricity came back on.

The three of them looked at one another, blinking, as though awakening from a harrowing dream. Charlotte darted a glance around the kitchen. Two broken mugs and a broken wine glass lay on the counter. All the cupboard doors remained open. Aunt Marina set the scissors gently down on the table. With a dainty finger she began counting the pieces of cut card. But Charlotte noticed her hand was shaking.

"Thirteen," she said.

"Is it gone?" whispered Lauren. "The curse, or whatever? Is it all cut out of the card?"

Aunt Marina smiled weakly. She drew in a ragged breath. "I don't really know, Lauren. I've never actually tried to exorcise a curse from a card before, if that's what this was. I'm kind of learning this as I go along." She stood up from her chair and began closing the cupboard doors one by one. Then she found a paper bag and began delicately picking up the broken shards on the counter, dropping them into the bag.

"Should we just throw away the pieces?" asked Charlotte. "Of the card, I mean."

Aunt Marina turned toward the pieces of card on the table and furrowed her brow. "I don't think so. I think perhaps the best thing to do is to return the card to where you found it."

"Return it? You mean to the library?" asked Charlotte.

Aunt Marina nodded. "Just in case. Just to be completely

sure that the circle is complete and the curse is returned to its origin. And I think you should do it, Charlotte."

"Without Lauren?"

Aunt Marina nodded again. "Yes, to replicate the time you found it." She carefully gathered up the pieces using a pair of ordinary kitchen tongs, and dropped them into a plastic bag. Charlotte noticed that Aunt Marina didn't want to touch the pieces of card even though their little ceremony was over. After rummaging around in the kitchen drawers, Aunt Marina found a small metal box, which had just a couple of mints left in it. These she took out, and dropped the plastic bag with the card pieces into the now-empty container. She clapped it shut and handed it to Charlotte.

"Is that it, then?" asked Charlotte in a small voice. "Is it over?"

Aunt Marina hesitated. "As I said, I haven't ever done anything like this before. But I think so. I hope so. Now. How about popcorn and a movie?"

"How about if we watch a musical tonight?" said Lauren. "Something really silly and fun."

"Sounds good to me," said Charlotte.

"Me too," agreed Aunt Marina.

CHAPTER 12

The next morning Charlotte stood on the front stoop of the library, shivering a little in the early chill, waiting for it to open. It was a few minutes before ten, the opening hour, but she seemed to be the only person eager to get in. It had been raining when she'd left Aunt Marina's house, so she'd borrowed an umbrella from her. Now, though, the atmosphere was eerily still. The sky had a strange, almost greenish tint to it, and unseasonably warm air had crept in. Where a minute before she'd been clutching her sweatshirt to herself and shivering, she now felt a trickle of sweat dribble down her stomach. Maybe that was nerves, though.

She slipped her hand into her jacket pocket and felt

the tin that contained the thirteen pieces of the card. She shuddered with dread. The sooner she got rid of these pieces of card the better.

"Oh, Charlotte, hello, good morning, good morning!" said Mrs. Lazer, limping hurriedly up the steps behind her and jangling her set of keys. "Am I late?"

"Good morning, Mrs. Lazer," said Charlotte, stepping to the side to let the librarian open up the building. "No, you're not late. I think I'm early. Um, how are you feeling? I heard you had a little accident."

"Oh, pshhh," scoffed Mrs. Lazer. "I'm getting better every day. It was just a sprain, and I still have no idea how I managed to step off that stool like that. Heaven knows I've been up and down that step stool hundreds of times before. But I'll be right as rain in another week or two."

"I'm so glad to hear that," said Charlotte, and she meant it. "I guess I'm here bright and early."

"You are, but that's a good thing," said Mrs. Lazer, still fumbling with the keys. "Although I'll be perfectly honest with you—I don't like the look of that wall of clouds over there." She pointed.

Charlotte swiveled around to observe the sky over the post office, where Mrs. Lazer had gestured. A huge, black cloud, almost vertical in shape, loomed over the western horizon. It *was* sort of eerie. To the east the sky was cloudless and blue.

"They're predicting high winds and heavy thunderstorms," continued Mrs. Lazer, banging open the heavy old door with her hip and holding it open for Charlotte to enter. She flicked on the lights from the master switch next to the front door, and the beautiful old library lit up. She made her way toward the reference desk in the children's room and set down her big bag. "If you don't mind, I'm going to keep my weather radio on near my desk."

"No, that's fine, of course," said Charlotte. "I'm just here to look for—um—a book."

"Do you need help finding it?"

"No!" said Charlotte, too quickly. "No, thanks, I'm good. I know which one I want."

Mrs. Lazer bustled around, picking up books to reshelve and flicking on area lights. Charlotte noticed Mrs. Lazer had a plastic brace on her ankle.

Charlotte headed straight for the shelf labeled HORROR. It was in the far area of the stacks, near the west wall. She was relieved to be out of Mrs. Lazer's sight line.

There was the red book, back in its place on the high shelf above her head. Peering around the corner to be sure Mrs. Lazer wasn't looking, she set down her overnight bag, dragged the footstool underneath the shelf with the red book, and stepped onto it. With a shaking hand she pulled the small tin from her pocket and opened it. Then she reached up and took the red book down from the shelf.

The pages seemed to crackle with something akin to static electricity as she slipped the first of the thirteen pieces of the card into the book. Carefully she closed the book and put it away. Her hands were still shaking, and it took several attempts to shove the book back into the space it had occupied on the shelf.

She could hear it start to rain again outside. It seemed to be the loudest rain she'd ever heard. It pattered like drumsticks on a snare drum.

"I think that's hail!" called Mrs. Lazer from across the huge room. Charlotte's view of her was blocked by the shelving, but she guessed they were still the only two in the library.

She climbed down from the stool—carefully—and then walked to the end of the row and stuck her head out. "Yeah, sounds like it," she called back.

"I think you'd better stay here until this storm passes, honey!" called Mrs. Lazer. "It sounds like a doozy!"

Charlotte nodded and quickly headed back to the place she'd just been. She had to do this fast, in case the power went out. And she had to be brave. For her father's sake. Her father was always at the back of her mind. His safety. His very life.

She began pulling other books off the shelf, books that were in the vicinity of the red one. One by one, from high shelves and low shelves, she selected books and then slipped the pieces of card between the pages. Each time she experienced that same sensation as she opened a book to insert the piece of card—a staticky crackle, like when you pulled two socks apart that had just come out of the dryer. She did this until the pieces were all gone. When she'd finished, she stood, staring at the shelf of books, breathing heavily. She hoped this would work. She hoped that once and for all she had gotten rid of this curse, or whatever it was the card had brought on her.

A new worry struck her. What if someone else checked out a book with one of the thirteen pieces? What if she was passing along bad luck to thirteen new people? She thought of the old movie she'd seen when she was a kid, the one where a sorcerer's broom kept dividing and dividing and as it did, it gained, rather than lost, strength. That movie had totally traumatized her. She'd slept between her parents for a week after watching it.

She stood, looking at the bookshelf, gnawing on her knuckle. Had this been a terrible mistake? She'd reproached Lauren for suggesting they pass the card to a really old person or to a really ill person. What if she'd just passed it to thirteen perfectly healthy members of the reading public? What if—

Her worried thoughts were interrupted by Mrs. Lazer calling her name.

"Charlotte! Come quick!"

She could hear the wind howling outside. She grabbed her overnight bag, slung it over her shoulder, scooted out of the stacks, and stopped. Her ears! They hurt! It brought back an awful memory from when she was eight years old—her mom had tried to teach her how to blow up and then tie a balloon when she'd been helping get ready for the twins' fourth birthday party. There'd been one particularly difficult balloon that refused to blow up, and Charlotte had popped her ears trying to blow into it. The memory of that pain came roaring back. Her ears felt the same way they'd felt then. She hunched her shoulders and pressed her ears with the heels of her hands.

"Never mind your ears! The radio is saying tornados might be touching down in our area!" called Mrs. Lazer, who had emerged from behind her desk. "We should go to the basement. Now!"

Charlotte broke into a run and followed Mrs. Lazer, who limped ahead of her, into the small vestibule of the library and toward a side door off the main entrance that she'd noticed a few times but had never opened. Mrs. Lazer unlocked it with shaking hands and held the door for her, flicking on the lights as she did so. Charlotte peered down a narrow flight of stairs leading to the library basement. Mrs. Lazer hustled Charlotte down and then followed her.

Down in the shadowy basement of the library the noise of the weather grew muffled. It smelled musty and damp, like old books. Through a narrow casement window close to the ceiling, Charlotte could see greenish light filtering in from outside.

Mrs. Lazer guided her, with a hand to her back, around bookcases full of books and toward the back of the vast room.

It was hot and stuffy. Charlotte loved the smell of old books, but down here it was overpowering.

"There's an old bathroom through here," said Mrs. Lazer, gesturing toward a heavy oak door standing slightly ajar. "No windows. I think it's probably the safest place for us."

They moved into the small bathroom, which contained an old-fashioned toilet—the kind with the tank mounted on the wall above and that you flushed by pulling on a chain. There was also an old-fashioned sink that had separate faucets for hot and cold, but nothing in the middle. The walls seemed to be made of marble or granite, and the floor was patterned with small, old-fashioned tiles.

Mrs. Lazer had brought along her battery-powered, portable radio, but the reception was fuzzy and staticky. Several agitated voices kept coming in and out, talking about high winds and touchdowns and other things Charlotte couldn't make out. "We'll just stay in here until we think the coast is clear," said Mrs. Lazer.

Charlotte nodded, wondering where her mother and brothers were right now. Their house had a basement. That was good. Were they at home? She hadn't even called to check in this morning before she'd headed from Lauren's house to the library.

There was nowhere to sit except on top of the closed lid of the toilet. Charlotte insisted Mrs. Lazer sit there, and Charlotte slid down the wall next to the sink until she was sitting on the floor.

They heard the roaring wind, which rapidly grew louder and louder like a huge locomotive bearing down on them. The lights went out, plunging them into darkness, but Charlotte was too afraid of what was happening outside to worry about being afraid of the dark. She felt Mrs. Lazer lean forward to clasp her hand and squeeze it. It was a reassuring kind of squeeze. She was glad Mrs. Lazer was there with her. But her mouth went dry from terror and every muscle in her body tensed. The roaring became so loud it was almost unbearable. Had Charlotte chosen to scream at the top of her lungs, Mrs. Lazer probably wouldn't have heard it, the roaring was that loud. With her back to the wall, Charlotte could feel the very building shaking and quivering. She thought again about her family and prayed that they were all right.

How much time elapsed while the roaring and the popping and the shaking of the entire building continued? It felt like half an hour. It was probably about a minute. But then everything went still. The roaring stopped almost as suddenly as it had started.

Charlotte realized she'd had her eyes squeezed tightly closed the whole time. Now she opened them. She couldn't see anything in the darkness, but a lighter patch of gray appeared, and she realized Mrs. Lazer had opened the bathroom door.

"Are you all right, sweetie?" she asked. She sounded out of breath, as though she'd just finished a race.

"Um, yes, fine," Charlotte replied in a high, tremulous voice.

"Watch your step now. It looks like some books have fallen down from their shelves."

They made their way through the dim basement. It was hard to see with the lights out, but now a somewhat brighter light filtered in through the small windows close to the ceiling. Charlotte was relieved to find that, at least on this side of the room, none of the windows were broken.

Mrs. Lazer led the way up the stairs, with Charlotte following cautiously behind.

The small entryway seemed fine. A picture had fallen off the wall but hadn't broken. Through the door leading into the library, Charlotte could see that the library seemed okay too. A few books were on the floor. *Maybe,* she thought with relief, *it hadn't been an actual tornado. Maybe it hadn't—*

Then they stepped inside and saw the whole room.

Charlotte's jaw dropped open. Next to her, Mrs. Lazer seemed unable to speak, any more than Charlotte could.

Along the west side of the library, toward the back, an entire section of wall was missing. Beyond the piles of rubble, dust, and books Charlotte could see green grass and bright sky, a bit of parking lot, and broken fence.

Piles of books had been thrown off their shelves and lay in haphazard heaps. One of the shelves had tipped on its side, spewing books onto the floor and against the shelf next to it. And one whole section of shelves was missing altogether. It had simply vanished.

"Look," breathed Mrs. Lazer, who seemed to have found her voice at last. "The horror section has blown clean away. Weren't you standing right there when the storm hit?" She clutched Charlotte's arm. "To think what might have happened." She shook her head in disbelief.

Charlotte looked. It was true. Where she had been standing—was it just five minutes before?—there was nothing left. Just a view to the sky, which was now clearing.

Her mind was a whirl of thoughts, fears, worries. She had to get home to find her family, to see if they were okay. She had to see if her house was okay. And then a thought popped into her mind.

The card.

The tornado must have taken it away. All thirteen pieces. The books were gone. The bits of card inside the books were gone. Had she, Charlotte, done this? Had she caused the tornado to come? To blow away part of the library?

She felt sick just thinking about it.

Mrs. Lazer had her ear to the radio, listening intently.

"Does your phone work, Charlotte?"

Her phone. Of course! She could call her mother. With trembling hands she turned it on.

No service.

"There's no service," she said. "I need to know if my

family is okay. Can I go now? It's only three blocks."

They could hear the wail of sirens in the distance.

Mrs. Lazer nodded, still listening to the radio. "I think it's all right now. The sky looks clear and blue. Yes, go. Be careful. I'm going to lock up and go see what's what with my own house too. Although it feels a little silly to lock the place, when there's a whole wall missing."

Charlotte took off running. She'd only just made it down the front steps of the library when she felt her phone buzz. Was cell service back?

She whipped it out of her jacket pocket. It was a message from the mysterious texter.

It's over. For now.

CHAPTER 13

Lauren staggered over with another huge box and deposited it on the table in front of Charlotte with a loud thump.

"Wow. More, huh?" said Charlotte, looking around for the scissors. "I think people have donated five times more books than the library actually lost in the tornado."

"I think you're right," said Lauren with a grin. She picked up the scissors that were behind the box she'd just brought over and handed them to her friend. Then she gestured with her chin toward the western wall of the main reading room. "And really, you'd never in a million years guess there'd been a tornado at all. Kind of amazing how quickly they repaired it."

"It really was bizarre how the only tornado damage happened here at the library," said Charlotte.

"Well, there were some barns that got damaged farther out of town," Lauren pointed out.

Charlotte nodded. "I know. But still."

Neither girl said anything more. But Charlotte was sure Lauren was thinking what she was thinking. That the damage from this tornado had been no coincidence.

"Hey, congratulations again about your father," said Charlotte, smiling at her friend.

"Thanks," said Lauren, grinning back. "I'm pretty psyched he got the grant. His research suddenly took a turn for the better. Funny how fortunes can change so quickly."

The two exchanged another look. Charlotte's phone buzzed. It was her mom.

She groaned. "Ugh. The Bianchis want me to babysit tonight. They live in that big, creepy house on the edge of town that has really crummy Internet service, and they're always later than they say they'll be."

"Don't they have twin girls?" asked Lauren.

"Yep," said Charlotte. "I think they think that since

I have twin brothers I'm the only babysitter capable of handling them. Which actually might be true. Those kids really are a handful." She shrugged. "I'll tell her yes, though. They pay well." She texted her mother back.

Mrs. Lazer came in, wheeling a hand truck stacked with three more boxes. "Look at all this!" she said happily. "From three different publishing companies, all the way from New York! You young people and your social networks! It's remarkable how well you two have spread the word about our rebuilding campaign!"

The girls smiled at each other, and then hurried over to help Mrs. Lazer unload the newest boxes.

"I'll need to leave the two of you to hold down the fort," said Mrs. Lazer, "while I go work on the accounting end of all this. If we're going to reopen next week, I have so much paperwork to get through!"

The girls assured her they had everything under control, and Mrs. Lazer left them.

"So, Char?" asked Lauren when they were by themselves again. "Do you think it was, you know, the card?"

They'd never talked about the card, not since the morning of the tornado, when Charlotte had left Lauren and Aunt Marina to head to the library.

Charlotte nodded. "Yes, I do think it was the card. It's too much of a coincidence. Why did it strike just after I'd stuck the thirteen pieces into those thirteen books? Why did it only touch down near the library and only carry away that particular section? Why were those books never found? It's just too weird."

"And look how our fortunes changed after that," said Lauren. "Teddy's fine." She ticked that off on her fingers. "The play went great. My dad got his grant. Stacy Matthews has actually decided we're not as uncool as she thought."

"That's true," said Charlotte, grinning. "She's been downright nice to the two of us recently. She even said happy birthday to me last week."

"Maybe now that you're a teenager, she thinks you're somewhat cooler," joked Lauren.

Charlotte smiled. "Maybe."

"And of course, your dad came home safe and sound a few days after the tornado," Lauren continued. "All that bad stuff that had been happening seemed to stop happening as soon as you got rid of the card."

"It does seem that your Aunt Marina was right," agreed Charlotte. "She said that the Wheel of Fortune card could change your fortune for worse or for better. It certainly seems like it's changed for the better . . . now that the curse is gone."

"Knock wood," said Lauren.

"Knock wood," said Charlotte, quickly rapping her knuckles on the table.

"Speaking of Teddy," said Lauren, glancing at the clock, "I need to run home and walk him and then get dressed for the banquet they're having for my dad. He's going to give a big presentation tonight. Are you okay by yourself here for a while?"

"Of course," said Charlotte with a laugh, shoving the big box to the side and picking up a brown envelope she hadn't noticed before. It was addressed to the library and marked BOOK DONATION.

"Okay, see ya soon," said Lauren, hopping down from her stool. "You want me to turn the radio on to keep you company?"

Charlotte grinned. "Mrs. Lazer is positive her little radio saved our lives with its tornado warning. She's probably right. Sure, you can turn it on."

Lauren grinned and switched it on and then headed out.

Charlotte reached for the letter opener—a fancy

word for what was actually a butter knife—and slit open the brown package just as the weather came on.

"No threat of tornadoes tonight, folks. But sleet and freezing rain begins later on tonight. And lots more snow in the forecast for the rest of the weekend."

She rolled her eyes as she slipped a small, leather-bound book out of the package. Why did there have to be sleet and freezing rain on a nonschool night? Such a waste of a potential school closing!

She glanced down at the book to check the title, in order to see which pile it should go in. She turned it over. The title wasn't visible anywhere, not even on the spine. The binding was old, dark-green leather, and the indecipherable lettering on its spine looked like it had once been embossed gold.

Suddenly her heart rate quickened. She was getting that feeling. The same feeling she'd gotten months before. The time when that red book had felt as though it was calling to her. This book was sending out a powerful message too. It was telling her to open it.

She dreaded what she might find, but her hands ignored her mind and opened up the book. Was it her imagination, or had she felt a slight crackling in the pages? She decided she'd just imagined it. Would she find another card? Or the same card, somehow miraculously restored to its original condition?

There seemed to be no card inside. That was a relief. The title, in old-fashioned type, was *A Girl's Life*. The book smelled musty, that old-book smell that Charlotte loved. It was almost intoxicating. The pages were silky soft and satisfyingly thick between her fingers as she turned to a random page and began to read, inhaling deeply as she did so:

Suddenly the girl sat up in bed and flicked the light back on. She had that feeling again—as though something was beckoning to her. But this time it wasn't the book. It was the thing that had fallen out of it. She felt an overwhelming need to find it and look at it. She swung her legs around and got out of bed. There it was. A stiff, cardboard card, sort of like a playing card except bigger, sturdier.

She picked it up and studied it. Weird.

In the center was a round orange shape, which looked sort of like a compass—

Charlotte slammed the book closed. Her heart walloped in her chest. Her hands shook so badly that she dropped the book onto the table. Almost move for move, the book described Charlotte's actions on the night she had discovered the card.

She picked up the envelope that the book had arrived in. Turned it over. No return address. The handwriting was eerily familiar though. It'd been a while, but she knew where she'd seen it before. The envelope had been addressed by the same hand that had written that message on the back of the card. There was no mistaking the old-fashioned, spidery lettering.

With trembling hands she picked up the book again. She flipped the pages slowly, carefully, until she got to about the midway point.

And then the pages became blank.

The last half of the book was completely, entirely blank.

The radio suddenly grew louder, although she hadn't gone anywhere near it.

"—no chance of tornadoes tonight, but stock up on those flashlights and batteries. There's gonna be a doozy of a storm, and we may lose power! Who knows what might happen in the dark?"

DO NOT FEAR—
WE HAVE ANOTHER CREEPY TALE FOR YOU!

TURN THE PAGE FOR A SNEAK PEEK AT

You're invited to a

CREEPOVER™

Off the Wall

"I don't want to go," Jane whispered to herself. "*I don't want to go.*"

Ahead of her the huge, cavernous lobby of the Templeton Memorial Museum was ringing with the clamor of fifty other girls Jane's age. They were lined up in front of a long table, eagerly signing in for the Templeton Lock-In. A poster on the wall above the tables blasted the neon-pink words: THRILL TO AN OVERNIGHT EXPERIENCE BEHIND THE SCENES OF THE MUSEUM! But from her place at the end of the line, Jane was not thrilled. Not one bit.

"It will be good for you," her mother had said to her that morning. "You need to socialize with more girls your own age."

But what, Jane wondered, *am I supposed to say to girls I've never seen before in my life? And how on earth can I possibly spend an entire sleepover with them?*

She cast a miserable glance around the lobby—a bustling hive of girls and their parents and all their random good-bye conversations.

"Dad, I don't *need* an alarm clock! They'll wake us up, I swear!" And "I don't see your allergy pillow, honey. Where's your allergy pillow?" And "*Fine,* then! I don't want to hear another word about it!" And "No, Mommy, don't hug me. Everyone will think I'm a baby."

I'm just not anything like these girls, Jane thought. *I can tell just by looking at them. Why, why did I have to—*

"Are you here to register, dear?" came the friendly voice of a woman in front of her.

Jane literally jumped out of her thoughts. The line had been moving along without her noticing, and now she was standing right at the registration table.

"I guess so," said Jane. Nervously she twisted a hank of her blond hair around one finger.

"Okay! What's your name?"

"Jane Meunier."

The woman glanced through a sheaf of papers and

checked off Jane's name. "Have you done a lock-in with us before, Jane?"

"No. We—I—uh—just moved here," Jane stammered. "I don't know anything about *anything*."

The woman chuckled. "Well, then, you are in for a wonderful surprise. This is going to be the best night of your life! Now, where's your sleeping bag?"

Jane pointed to a pile of blankets in her basket.

"Oh, no sleeping bag?" remarked the woman. "Did you bring a foam pad to put under your blankets? That floor can feel awfully hard."

"Foam pad?" exclaimed Jane. "I've never heard of using a foam pad! Oh, I *knew* this was going to be bad!"

"Don't look so worried!" said the woman. "They've got extra foam mattresses in the Great Hall for people who need them. And you'll have a wonderful time. The lock-in is one of our most popular events. There's a huge waiting list every time."

"She's right. The lock-in is really, really fun." This voice was coming from in back of Jane. She turned around to see that the girl behind her—who had dark hair and brown eyes—was smiling at her. "I'm so excited!" the girl continued. "I've been waiting to be old enough ever since my sister did a lock-in here three years ago. Hi, Mrs. Crawford," she added. "I guess you know I'm here to register."

"Yes indeedy, Lucy," said the woman at the table. "I've got your paperwork right here! Jane, this is Lucy Nasim. Lucy has attended every single Templeton Museum event in the history of the world."

"That's pretty much true," said Lucy. "Pottery workshops, plant hunts in the park, Meet the Owls—you name it. I *love* this museum. I totally wish I *lived* here."

Jane smiled shyly at Lucy. At this moment, she wasn't exactly feeling the same way, but she could already tell that Lucy was really nice.

Mrs. Crawford handed each girl a name tag. "Lucy, this is Jane's first time at the museum. Why don't you take her to the Great Hall? The group leaders are already there. And help her get a foam mattress, okay?"

"Of course I will," said Lucy, shouldering her backpack.

"And Lucy—none of your practical jokes tonight, okay?" Mrs. Crawford turned to Jane and said, "Lucy can be kind of a prankster. Don't let her play any tricks."

Lucy rolled her eyes in mock exasperation. "I'll try to be good. Let's go, Jane. I know *everything* about this museum," she added with a laugh as they began walking.

"The Great Hall's where we're going to be sleeping. It's down at the far end of the building. I think the museum people put it there because they like you to walk past some of their greatest hits on the way."

"Greatest hits?"

"Oh, you know, like some of the most famous stuff. There's a pearl the size of a baseball, for instance. And what some people think might have been King Arthur's crown. And in there is the Hall of Mythology," said Lucy. "It's super popular."

In the center of that gallery, a marble boy was struggling to free himself from the tentacles of a massive marble sea serpent. Behind the sea serpent, Jane could see a wall mosaic of a ten-foot-tall woman who seemed to have snakes for hair. And next to the snake-haired woman, even taller, was a battered wooden statue of some kind of monster with not one but three ferocious dog heads.

"Those myths can get pretty weird," Lucy said cheerfully. "But I guess people like the exhibit—it's always crowded."

The crowd was thinning out now that the museum was about to close. People were hurrying past the girls on their way toward the lobby, and as Jane and Lucy passed the next exhibit hall, the lights blinked off. Glancing back, Jane realized that the mythology gallery was also dark now. For some reason, she didn't like the thought of that sea serpent and the snake-haired woman standing silent and motionless in a darkened room.

"Ta-da! Here's the Great Hall!" Lucy exclaimed.

The Great Hall was a huge round chamber with a vaulted ceiling so high above the girls' heads that Jane wasn't sure she could actually see the top. As they walked in, Jane noticed that the hall had four identical entryways spaced at equal intervals, like the directions on a compass. She and Lucy were passing through the south entrance. It had an old-looking map of the south pole over the door, but that was the only thing that distinguished it from the other three entrances.

"I always go in through this door," said Lucy. "I love Antarctica."

But Jane wasn't paying attention. She was staring into the Great Hall, which was now full of excited girls. Some were laying out their sleeping bags and arranging pillows on top of them. Some were studying the murals lining the curved walls. Some were standing around chatting in groups of three or four. And all of them were shouting at the top of their lungs—or that's how it seemed to Jane.

"There's Lucy! *Loooocy!* LOOOOCEEEEEYYY!" someone screamed, and a girl with curly red hair and round blue eyes raced up to them.

"I was beginning to wonder when you were going to get here," the girl panted. She looked over at Jane. "Hey, who's this?"

"This is Jane. It's her first time here," Lucy answered. "Jane, this is Cailyn. She goes to school with me."

Cailyn tossed Jane a quick smile and instantly launched into a long description of her summer. "And then we went to the Silver Islands and I learned how to water ski and almost broke my leg, but it turned out to be a sprain, but I think a sprain hurts even more, and then I went to camp for two weeks and I got *the* most horrible sunburn you ever saw, and then my brother and I went to my aunt's farm in Danville . . ."

"*Lucy!* I've missed you so much!" Another girl had just rushed up, and two others followed her. *Is everyone here a friend of Lucy's?* Jane wondered. Within a couple of minutes, she and Jane were surrounded by a cluster of excited girls.

About twenty conversations seemed to be going on at

once. Jane did her best to keep up. All these girls seemed pretty nice, she realized. Probably kids who *wanted* to spend a night in a museum were interesting and fun.

There was one girl in the group, Megan, who seemed to be even more nervous than Jane. "These floors are awfully slippery," she told Jane earnestly right after they'd been introduced. "We're going to have to walk *very* carefully. I made sure to wear shoes that have a lot of traction."

So yes, it was probably safe to say that Megan was scared too. Also, Jane reminded herself, she *couldn't* be the only shy person in a group of fifty girls. What about that girl hanging back at the outer edge of the group, for instance? The one with the straight black hair and the sour expression? She looked sort of scared, sort of stuck up, and sort of, well, angry, Jane decided. But what was there to be mad about?

Abruptly the girl seemed to realize that Jane was looking at her. She glared back at Jane, her eyes narrowed.

Jane felt bad for being rude. She gave the girl an embarrassed smile.

But the girl didn't smile back. If anything, she seemed to get even angrier.

I dare you to speak to me, her look was conveying. *I dare you.*

WANT MORE CREEPINESS?

Then you're in luck because P. J. Night has
some more scares for you and your friends!

What Scares You?

In this story, Charlotte and Lauren come face-
to-face with some of their biggest fears because of
the mysteriously cursed tarot card. What are your
biggest fears? Write them in the thirteen spaces
below. Feel free to ask your friends to contribute
their biggest fears to fill in all the spaces!

1. _____
2. _____
3. _____
4. _____
5. _____
6. _____
7. _____
8. _____
9. _____
10. _____
11. _____
12. _____
13. _____

Bonus Activity: How many times does P. J. Night use the word "thirteen" in this story? How many can you find?

_____

YOU'RE INVITED TO . . .
CREATE YOUR OWN SCARY STORY!

Do you want to turn your sleepover into a creepover? Telling a spooky story is a great way to set the mood. P. J. Night has written a few sentences to get you started. Fill in the rest of the story and have fun scaring your friends.

You can also collaborate with your friends on this story by taking turns. Have everyone at your sleepover sit in a circle. Pick one person to start. She will add a sentence or two to the story, cover what she wrote with a piece of paper leaving only the last word or phrase visible, and then pass the story to the next girl. Once everyone has taken a turn, read the scary story you created together aloud!

At first I didn't think much of the e-mail my best friend sent me. After all, it was only a chain letter, and those things don't mean anything, right? And even though the letter claimed that if I didn't forward it to thirteen people, thirteen horrible things would happen to me within thirteen days, I pressed delete and went to bed. But the bad luck started the very next day when I fell asleep on the school bus and missed my stop. The day after that was worse. I tripped in the cafeteria and broke my leg—in front of my entire school. And then things went from bad to horrifying. On day three . . .

_____

_____

_____

_____

_____

_____

_____

_____

_____

THE END

A lifelong night owl, **P. J. NIGHT** often works furiously into the wee hours of the morning, writing down spooky tales and dreaming up new stories of the supernatural and otherworldly. Although P. J.'s whereabouts are unknown at this time, we suspect the author lives in a drafty, old mansion where the floorboards creak when no one is there and the flickering candlelight creates shadows that creep along the walls. We truly wish we could tell you more, but we've been sworn to keep P. J.'s identity a secret . . . and it's a secret we will take to our graves!

Did you **LOVE** this book?

Want to get access to great books for **FREE?**

Join

Simon & Schuster IN THE bookloop

where you can

Read great books for FREE!

Get exclusive excerpts

Chat with your friends

Log on to join now!

everloop.com/loops/in-the-book